PENGUIN BOOKS

# LOOKING AFTER THE ASHES

Kopi Soh is the pseudonym of a US based Malaysian author and illustrator best known for her book *Oh, I Thought I Was The Only One*. She founded the Facebook community 'Stick It To Me', currently renamed 'Kopi Soh's Positive Healing Doodles', an initiative centred around producing 'healing art' for the terminally sick and needy, and organizes a group of volunteers to produce art for hospitals and charities. Her work with 'Stick It To Me' was recognized in the Digi WWWOW Awards 2015, winning an award in the Social Gathering category. She also served as the official illustrator for TEDxWeldQuay 2013.

Kopi Soh was also a former manager with a women's centre, training social workers and counsellors. She counsels victims in Domestic Violence situations and children who have been sexually assaulted. Being a crisis counsellor she was also a Sexual Assault Team Responder for the County of San Diego and in her spare time she teaches social media at a community school for the elderly. Her area of specialty is in working with children, adolescents, couples, seniors, refugees, rape victims, abused kids, victims of domestic violence and families.

Kopi Soh's first book, *Oh, I Thought I Was The Only One*, published by Dawning Victory Consultancy in 2012, distributed by MPH, is a self-help book oriented towards creating awareness of common psychological issues, which manifest in daily life. In 2013, Kopi Soh published her second book, *Oh . . . I Thought I Was the Only One 2*, a sequel focusing on how children experience various stresses in their daily lives and teaching them skills on how to overcome them.

Kopi Soh has been accepted into a doctoral program for the year 2020. Her proposed research will be about Flourishing, Happiness and Older Malaysian Women.

# Looking After the Ashes

*Old Wives' Tales, Taboos, Supernatural and Childhood Superstitions*

Kopi Soh

PENGUIN BOOKS

An imprint of Penguin Random House

PENGUIN BOOKS

USA | Canada | UK | Ireland | Australia
New Zealand | India | South Africa | China | Southeast Asia

Penguin Books is part of the Penguin Random House group of companies
whose addresses can be found at global.penguinrandomhouse.com

Published by Penguin Random House SEA Pte Ltd
9, Changi South Street 3, Level 08-01,
Singapore 486361

First published in Penguin Books by Penguin Random House SEA 2021

Illustration credits KULit Baru

ISBN 9789814882101

Typeset in Adobe Garamond Pro by Manipal Technologies Limited, Manipal

www.penguin.sg

# Contents

# Preface

*If you eat while lying down, you will turn into a snake...*

*If you don't polish off all the rice on your plate you will marry a man full of pimples and pockmarks.*

Growing up in a large extended Peranakan family filled with strong women, I hear these words of 'wisdom' daily. I used to live in a world where clipping nails at night was strictly prohibited, pointing at the moon would result in one's ears getting chopped off, and children were forced to stay indoors during sundown for fear of collision with evil forces.

The title 'Looking after the Ashes' (Piara Abu) is derived from the word, *Piara* (pelihara in Malay), which means 'to keep and look after', and while *Abu* literally means 'ash' in Malay, it is the Baba term for ancestor. So *Piara Abu,* as a whole, refers to 'looking after the ashes/ancestors'—something that directly corresponds to the custom of installing a permanent altar for regular domestic worship.

Then there is the ritual of inviting the deceased to return to be worshipped. This practice is called *chnia abu* or 'inviting the ancestors': *Chnia* is a Hokkien word, which means 'to invite'.

The Cheah family's story is not your typical 'Chinese from China' story; although our unique subgroup is considered

'Chinese', we don't speak the language. For me, Swee Lian's tale is an important one to tell because my people, the Baba-Nyonyas (Peranakans) are slowly fading. This subculture has lost itself, even among its own people. I guess you could call us the 'Brigadoonians' of South East Asia—people who find themselves keepers of ancient customs and traditions that were long discarded, even in Mainland China.

I do wish to share with you the history of the Penang Peranakans. However, I personally think they are somewhat ambiguous although there are various claims as to how this subculture came to be. I am a tad bit suspicious (due to lack of concrete documented data) that we are descendants of the Princess Hang Li Po, the daughter of a Ming Emperor sent over to be the bride of Sultan Mansur Shah (r. 1459–1477). Other literature claims that we are a product of intermarriage. Once again, I question its validity; intermarriage is not a new concept and Chinese people emigrated all over the world. Why has that never produced a new culture before?

Other theories speculated that our ancestors were Hokkien seafarers who arrived and settled in the 15th, 16th and 17th centuries. We then chose to cut ourselves off from mainland China, thus going through a period of isolation resulting in the creation of our own unique traits and colourful fusion of culture by absorbing local folk beliefs and customs, mixing our Hokkien language with borrowed Malay words. Regardless of how we came to be, the Penang Peranakans flourished until the Mid-20th century. During the colonial era we were even called the 'King's Chinese'.

However, our community started declining during the Japanese occupation (1942–45) in Malaya (now Malaysia). In the ravages of war, many Peranakan families fell into poverty and debt, forcing them to sell off family heirlooms. During this time, daughters were also hurriedly married off to non-Peranakans, thus eroding our identity.

Today, the future of our language and culture hangs in the balance. To ensure the continued existence of these people, I would like to tell their stories through this book.

However, the recollection of the customs and taboos are meant solely to amuse and entertain. It is not meant as an educational resource. There may be slight discrepancies and differences in how each family practises the Peranakan culture depending on their location.

Kopi Soh
January 2020

This book is a 'legacy' I would like to leave for my son, Ian Lim. Ever since he was a little boy, he would ask me to share with him stories of my childhood in Malaysia. Even though he was born in Canada he had always had an interest in learning about his Malaysian roots.

I would also like to thank him for spending hours of his time, helping me edit, proofread and giving me valuable feedback on my manuscript, reading about things that were very foreign to him. Thank you for keeping my stories from wandering too far off track.

Your love, support and faith in me have inspired me to continue writing whenever I feel like giving up.

Thank you and with love always,

Mom

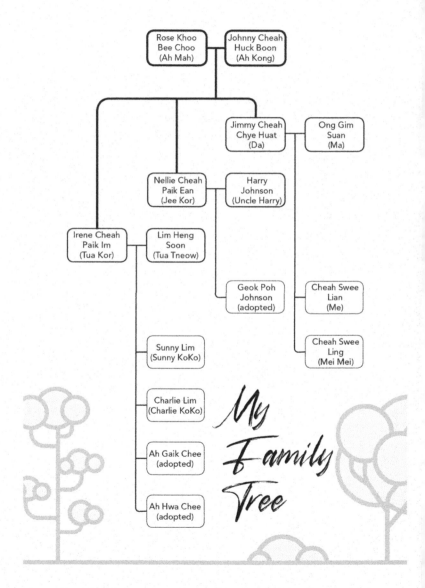

Rose Khoo
Bee Choo
(Ah Mah)

Johnny Cheah
Huck Boon
(Ah Kong)

Jimmy Cheah
Chye Huat
(Da)

Ong Gim
Suan
(Ma)

Nellie Cheah
Paik Ean
(Jee Kor)

Harry
Johnson
(Uncle Harry)

Irene Cheah
Paik Im
(Tua Kor)

Lim Heng
Soon
(Tua Tneow)

Geok Poh
Johnson
(adopted)

Cheah Swee
Lian
(Me)

Cheah Swee
Ling
(Mei Mei)

Sunny Lim
(Sunny KoKo)

Charlie Lim
(Charlie KoKo)

Ah Gaik Chee
(adopted)

Ah Hwa Chee
(adopted)

*My Family Tree*

# 1

# If You Are Ugly, It's a Boy . . .

From the moment of my genesis, I was surrounded by superstitions. My sex was supposedly determined by my mother's age and the month in which I was conceived. My parents had, in their efforts to conceive a boy, been eating lots of tofu, mushrooms, lettuce and carrots. As instructed, they had dutifully stayed away from foods such as pickles, meat and fish that were believed to result in the conception of a female fetus. In spite of their best efforts and my mom stuffing herself blue with tofu and mushrooms, which she hated, I was still born a girl.

Before I go on any further, let me introduce you to my family. Let's start with the woman who brought me into this world—my mother. My mother, Ma, was much like any other Asian woman; standing at a mere 5 feet tall, she was a petite 98 lb. woman with a soft voice and a shy reserved manner. Whenever she spoke, her watermelon seed-shaped face would tilt slightly toward the ground, and she seldom made eye contact. When she was born, people in her hometown, a small fishing village in the east coast of Peninsula Malaysia, called her *Cik Mek Puteh*, which meant 'Little Miss White.' It was quite a fitting name, for she did have a smooth fair skin, a pale milky yellow colour that resembled the skin of the langsat fruit.

Being the youngest in a family of seven, she was (for the most part) content to stay in the shadows of her elder, more boisterous, sisters and brothers. Similarly, when she married my father, she was quite content to stay in the shadows of his sisters, and she was most overshadowed by my Tua Kor, my father's eldest sister. Mind you, Tua Kor was not a loud woman, but somehow her imposing presence always commanded attention. She was a tall woman and big-boned too, yet always managed to look graceful in her cheongsam. Perhaps the most memorable thing about her was how she carefully tucked her handkerchief into the right shoulder of her blouse.

My father's second sister, my Jee Kor, was the complete opposite of her elder sister. Her two most memorable talents were holding one-sided conversations and pinching people with her toes. This bright-eyed, buck-toothed woman moved around like she was being propelled by a whirlwind, stopping only to sprinkle some criticism around, followed by a dash of advice. Yet she seldom stayed long enough to hear a complete sentence.

But enough about my aunts for now, let's move our focus back to my mother. My mother was a very intelligent woman, although she hardly ever expressed any opinion of her own. She learned to speak many languages merely by watching subtitled soap operas. If you were to ask me what the most memorable thing about her was, I would tell you that there are many, many things, but if I had to name one, it would be that she could repair any broken-down appliance as good as any electronics repairman could. However, while she was smart, she was also young and naive when she married my dad, and this made her prone to believing just about everything that her older sisters-in-law told her.

So when my aunts came home after visiting some friends on a humid July afternoon (though all the afternoons were humid regardless of the month) claiming that they could accurately predict the sex of her baby by merely looking at the shape of her pregnant belly, she believed them.

'Hello, hello, anybody home? Faster, open the door, very *juak* outside, so hot lah.' That was my Jee Kor; her voice often preceded her wherever she went, and this time was no exception.

Close behind Jee Kor was the imposing figure of Tua Kor, standing at 5 foot 6 inches.

'You never stop complaining, hot you complain, cold you complain, yesterday when it drizzled you made such a big deal of it, saying you need to go home immediately and wash your hair, otherwise you would fall sick. And I was in the midst of shopping for groceries,' said Tua Kor in a voice that, you knew, meant she was trying to be patient and not create a scene or solicit anymore backtalk from Jee Kor.

As she entered, she handed a packet of herbal medicine to my Ma. 'Here take this, Ah Suan, it's to ensure that you have an easy birth.'

As my Ma approached to take the packet, both Tua Kor and Jee Kor started poking and examining her stomach.

'You think it looks round?' Jee Kor asked Tua Kor.

'Hmm, Ah Suan, can you turn to the side? Let me have a look,' Tua Kor said as she looked carefully at the shape of my Ma's belly from all angles. 'I am not sure from this angle,' she turned my mother to the left, 'it looks round, but if she turns the other way, it looks a little pointy.'

'Hmm, I am really not sure now.' She wrinkled her brow, apparently perplexed.

Both my aunts were convinced that if my Ma's belly were round, I would be born a girl and if it were pointy, I would be born a boy. Since they were unable to determine if Ma's belly was round or pointy, they decided to resort to alternative methods of prediction. According to my aunts, my sex could also be predicted just by looking at my mother's features during her pregnancy.

'Ahhhh, your nose is big and red, therefore you'll have a boy, it's confirmed,' Tua Kor commented, expecting my mother to feel pleased in spite of feeling insulted. I guess in those days, since a woman was supposed to feel like she had been given the ultimate gift if she was carrying a boy, she should also feel happy and proud if her nose resembled Rudolph's big red nose.

'No, I think she's having a girl,' Jee Kor chimed in confidently, reexamining my mother's belly as though she were a trained physician. 'Look, how round her belly is!'

'Aiya, you always think you know everything, last time you made us all put chilli outside so that it won't rain. It rained anyway,' Tua Kor reminded Jee Kor irritably. Putting chilli outside was a well-known method in our family to deter the rain. As kids, whenever an outing was planned such as a visit to the beach or the botanical gardens, we would place a chilli on a stick and put it outside to make sure it didn't rain. Sometimes it worked, sometimes it didn't, but we did it anyway.

The debate between my aunts went on like this for hours, my mother barely saying a word all this time.

My paternal aunts made their predictions with such conviction that you might think the invention of the ultrasound machine had been a total waste of time. Eventually they left, retiring to their own rooms for a nap, undoubtedly pleased with the wisdom and insights they'd imparted to my grateful mother (who nevertheless remained no wiser than before about the sex of her child).

While carrying me, my poor mother was subject to many taboos, which were designed to protect her and the baby from 'malign influences.' At the time, it certainly seemed very important for my mother to follow these customs and superstitions to avert problems in pregnancy and childbirth such as miscarriages, stillbirth, and imperfections in the newborn.

For instance, she was prohibited from working with glue and other adhesives, lest the baby gets stuck coming out of the womb. Eating squid and crab was also forbidden because the former was believed to cause the uterus to 'stick' during delivery and the latter to result in a mischievous child. Even rubbing the abdomen too often was frowned upon since the result would be a spoilt and overly demanding child.

Most importantly, arguments and disputes were to be avoided at all costs because they were thought to be distressing to the baby (this I believe might prove to be true, according to recent research, intense or prolonged anger during pregnancy may lead to distress in the unborn child).

However, this 'no-argument rule' was a difficult one for my parents to abide by because my father, Da, was the complete opposite of my Ma, and they often fought because of their differences. While my mother was a woman of few words, my father was one of those people who could sell sand to people living in the desert. Even the way they ate was different. My mother preferred to eat with her hands, scooping up rice and curry with her right thumb and four fingers, while my father was brought up using a fork and spoon for his meals.

Coming from an affluent family, my father also brought with him a 'man of the world' demeanour. In contrast to my mother's lack of confidence, my father was (perhaps too) self-assured with his dark Eurasian good looks and muscular physique.

He was a man who looked tough outside but was as soft on the inside as a piece of tofu. Tall, dark and handsome with broad shoulders—that's how he looked in his pictures when he was younger. He liked to give things to people. You might say, 'Oh, so he was a generous man,' and I would answer you, 'I am not sure.' The thing with my dad was that he would give you things regardless of whether you wanted them or not. As long as he thought you needed them, he would buy them for you. Note that he wasn't a rich man by any means—he just found so much joy in giving, and so he bought, and he gave. But because I love him and in my eyes he can do very little wrong, I choose to believe that he has this uncanny ability of giving you those things that even you yourself don't realize you need. Once again, yes, that is what I choose to believe.

My father was also brought up in a very British manner, and the Chinese subgroup his family comes from, called the Baba-Nyonyas or Peranakans, is very different from the other Chinese groups.

'Da, why do we not speak in Mandarin?' I asked my father one morning as I watched him slathering Brylcreem on his hair, plastering it all down as he got ready for work.

'Well, only the low-class Chinese, those who come straight off the boat from China, speak in Mandarin. We are locally born sons of the soil—we are not immigrants.' My Da held his head up proudly as he explained.

Later on, I discovered that not just my father, but my entire family and all my relatives had no interest in learning how to write or speak the Chinese language. I myself grew up speaking only English and Hokkien, a dialect of Chinese.

It became quite apparent later on in life that the Peranakans thoroughly disliked and often looked down upon their China-born counterparts, calling them names like 'country bumpkins,' 'Chinaman hillbillies" and 'low class guests.' Unfortunately, these were the prejudices and racist attitudes of the times.

In spite of our biases, we Peranakans are a very colourful people with our own unique identity, customs and culture. We are often seen as refined, genteel, wealthy, educated and elite. Again, unlike the China-born Chinese immigrants who take low-class jobs such as fishing, mining, and tailoring, the Babas often become professional doctors, lawyers and architects.

I know at the beginning I said I was going to introduce you to my family. Well, I changed my mind. There are just too many people in my family. Besides my parents and their siblings, there's my grandparents, my cousins, my aunts, my uncles, and the *char bor kan* (servant maids), and yes, we all lived in the same house. So, I suppose I will just introduce them on a need-to-know basis, as and when my story requires.

# 2

# The Phoenix Goes with the Phoenix

As I mentioned earlier, my father and mother are the epitome of 'opposites attract'. Somehow the two of them managed to fall in love in spite of their many differences in status, personality and culture, not to mention the fierce objections from both families.

When my father first brought my mother home to visit his family, she was not welcomed with open arms. In fact, his family was quite unhappy, for my grandparents had already arranged for him a daughter of a rich shipping merchant. Marriage in my parents' day was viewed as an investment, a way of increasing your wealth, a union of convenience and profit rather than love. The motto of the rich Baba-Nyonyas was: 'The Phoenix goes with the Phoenix, the Hunchback with the coconut shoot.' Fortunately for me, this 'money marry money' mentality did not sit well with my father. He had found the girl of his dreams and he was prepared to stand by her.

One evening during one of their dates, my father confided in my mother. 'Did you know that I always wanted to join the army and be a soldier, but my family forbade it?'

'No I did not, I am so sorry to hear that,' Ma replied gently, shaking her head as she reached out to hold his hand.

'Following their wishes I became a businessman, taking after my father's business,' continued my Da as he looked sadly into my Ma's eyes. 'But you, you are way too important to me, and this time they will not get their way. My family can object all they want. They can even disown me. I will never give you up.'

And so after a few months of courtship, they secretly got engaged.

Because the engagement was so sudden and the wedding was to be held in just a couple of months, my aunts complained bitterly about their 'irresponsible' brother. Unlike my grandparents who were merely unhappy about my Da's choice of his partner, my aunts were more upset that he had not given them enough time to prepare for the wedding.

'This is very typical of Jimmy. *Boh hae lok*, sigh, so irresponsible,' complained my Tua Kor to my Jee Kor. My Jee

Kor, then *hair hoay* (literally, 'add fire'), instigated further, by adding, 'Yes, always want to *pang sai liao ka lai choai jamban,* do everything last minute.'

'I wonder if she put a love charm on him,' pondered my Tua Kor. 'You know these east coast women are famous for putting charms on unsuspecting men.'

This was an undeniable legend, if it was also possibly a myth. Throughout my life, I was told that East Coast women, especially women of Siamese descent like my mother, were adept in the black arts. In order to entice the man of her choice, the woman would seek help of a charm-maker to obtain a 'love spell' or 'love-object' that, when placed on her body, would make her beautiful and desirable to that man.

If this failed, the woman would then resort to a second method of casting her spell over the man. She would disrobe herself completely, stand naked with her legs straddled over a pot of steaming rice, and allow the sweat between her legs to trickle into the pot. The rice would then be served to the man, and it was believed that after eating it, he would forever be bound to her and abide by all her wishes.

'I really don't think that's the case. We all know how Jimmy is, so selfish, always thinking only of himself,' said Jee Kor, reluctant to entertain Tua Kor's suggestion.

For if they believed that my mother had put a love charm over my father, then my aunts would also be forced to accept that she had the power to put a hex on them if they were to oppose the union.

Women of Siamese descent were known for their vengeful nature. They would not hesitate to get rid of their enemies via cruel, torturous methods. This concoction of magic charms often consisted of lethal substances such as ground-up glass mixed with the hair and/or fingernails of the victim. The substance was then secretly added into the victim's meal, and once ingested, it would induce vomiting and hemorrhaging, eventually guaranteeing a slow and excruciating death.

'Maybe she's pregnant,' said my Jee Kor in a conspiratorial whisper. 'We have to find a way to expose her.'

'Shhhhh … don't let Ah Mak hear you say that,' cautioned Tua Kor, referring to my grandmother.

She knew that my grandma would have a fit at the hint of a possible scandal. Coming from a wealthy family, she was obsessed with keeping up appearances and saving face. Having a soon-to-be daughter-in-law pregnant out of wedlock would definitely create talk around the town and bring shame to the whole Cheah clan. Furthermore, my grandfather was a prominent figure in this town. He was the chairman of the

Cheah Kongsi (society), president of the Penang Club and vice president of the Chinese Businessman Association.

'What should we do then?' asked Jee Kor uncertainly, looking around to make sure that my grandmother was nowhere around.

'What about we make her wear a tight cheongsam,' suggested Tua Kor, 'that way she can't hide anything? If she's pregnant her belly would definitely show.'

I don't know if they had carried out their plan to expose my mother, but I didn't arrive until two years later.

By this time, my father's family, especially my paternal grandmother, my Ah Mah, had grown to love their talented, hardworking and good-natured daughter-in-law.

According to my Ma, she knew what my Da's family thought about her, and thus made up her mind to work hard and be the most filial daughter-in-law to my grandmother, the matriarch of the family. She was also determined to make her sisters-in-law love her.

'Everyday I would make sure I was the first to wake up,' said Ma during one of her before-bedtime storytelling sessions. 'I would take a quick shower, get dressed and then take the laundry out to the back patio to wash.'

'I had to put all the laundry into a big steel tub and then brush and scrub each one on a wooden washing board,' Ma explained. 'After the scrubbing I would put it into another big steel tub filled with clean water. From there I would rinse from one tub to another until the clothes were clean and no longer soapy, then I would take them out, wring them and hang them up to dry. By this time the morning sun would have been at just the right height to dry the clothes.'

'It must have been hard,' I said, imagining my Ma doing everything by hand.

'Once you get used to it, it is not so bad. The hardest part is when the sarongs needed to be starched and those can get pretty messy and tiring. Wringing a heavily starched sarong is hard work,' Ma replied.

'After laundry did you get to rest?' I asked with concern as I patted my Ma's arm lovingly.

'Haha, no … not really.' After some thought she added, 'I guess I could if I wanted to, but there was always so much work to be done in the kitchen so I thought I would make myself useful there. Normally after laundry was done, your Ah Mah and Ah Kong would have just returned from their morning shopping with baskets full of fresh ingredients for us to prepare lunch. Your aunts would be in charge of making the curries.'

'What about preparing the chicken?' I asked, hoping my Ma had not been tasked with slaughtering them.

'The servants were the ones to slaughter the chicken, cut up the fish and devein the prawns,' answered my Ma, much to my relief.

'What did you do then?'

'My task was to clean and wash the vegetables. Making sure I picked out all the rotten and yellowing ones and washed off all the sand and dirt before cutting. Depending on the dish, we had to cut those in different shapes. For example when we cooked the Nyonya Chap Chai, a mixed vegetable stew made up of Chinese cabbage, Chinese mushrooms, black fungus, lily flower bud, bean curd and carrots, your Ah Mah would always insist that the carrots be cut into a flower shape.'

'If you did something wrong would Ah Mah *cubit* you?' I had sometimes seen my grandma and my aunts pinching the servants when they did not do things the 'proper' way. I was afraid they would do the same to my mother.

'No, thank goodness I have never been pinched before for any wrongdoing,' Ma said with a smile.

'Do you get to cook the curries?' we suddenly heard Geok Poh, my Jee Khor's adopted daughter, asking. Geok Poh was a small-sized, bespectacled girl with thick glasses and a mass of bushy hair. We sometimes called her *hor chio liap*, peppercorn, because although she was small, she was very smart and cunning. Often if there was an argument between two parties, she would utter words that would incite and inflame the two arguing parties even more.

She also has this uncanny ability to be stealthy and often appear out of nowhere. Apparently, she had been standing at the door listening to Ma's stories too.

Ma motioned for her to come in and join us. 'No, usually the curries and stews were cooked by your aunts or Uncle Ong, our family *chong poh*, the household Hainanese cook. And your grandma would oversee the mixing of the spices, making sure that everything had the right consistency and taste.'

My Ma's efforts to make her mother-in-law love her must have paid off, because when she was pregnant with me, my Ah Mah made a big fuss over her, ordering the servants to make nutritious foods and herbal soups for her. Throughout my mother's pregnancy, my Ah Mah looked after her like a mama bear watches over her cub.

'Make sure there are no pineapples in the dishes,' my Ah Mah instructed the servants sternly before turning to my Ma and explaining, '*sharp* fruits like that can cause miscarriage. Also don't take papaya.'

My appearance was supposedly predetermined by what my mother and father did during the pregnancy. If my mother ate lots of eggs, I would have skin as smooth and fair as an egg but lo and behold, if she ate lots of beef, I would be born as hairy as a monkey.

'If you don't believe me, look at all the white people, the *angmor kau,*' my Tua Kor would say in her *I-know-everything-so-you-better-believe-me* voice. 'They're so hairy because their mothers ate beef.'

All of us knew that when she referred to 'all the white people' or *angmor kau* (red-haired monkey, the term used to refer to Westerners), she meant my Jee Kor's husband who was an exceptionally hairy Englishman whose name also happened to be Harry. Our Uncle Harry was perhaps the only white person that my Tua Kor knew.

Each morning my mother would sullenly down her half-boiled eggs dipped in a few teaspoons of soy sauce. 'Why do I have to eat these disgusting slimy eggs?' she would complain to the maids while trying to wash the taste of the eggs off with her soy milk, a drink that she abhorred as well.

'Ah Suan, you know you have to drink lots of soybean milk so that your baby can be fair and chubby.' That was my grandmother's way of offering comfort to my mother.

On rare occasions my mother protested, hoping that the matriarch would let her off the hook, but when it came to ensuring the birth of healthy grandchildren—especially grandsons—my grandmother seldom compromised.

'I don't know-lah, if you don't want to drink, don't drink,' my grandma would reply in as off-hand a manner as she could manage. 'Don't blame me if your baby came out skinny and dark. Remember your cousin Sally Chee's baby, dark and skinny because she drinks lots of coffee when pregnant, also never drink soy milk.'

'Okay, Okay, I'll drink some,' sighed my mother looking at the off-white milky substance that was placed in front of her with disgust. But not wanting to bear the responsibility for my 'ugly looks,' she drank it anyway.

Sad, isn't it, how the traditional Chinese society blames the mother if her child is born with physical disabilities or is deformed in some way? Imperfections in the child are believed to have resulted from the mother's actions during pregnancy. I've heard that in some cases, infanticide is performed to spare the mother from shame, public humiliation and ostracism by their in-laws. In this case, I don't think my mother would have been ostracized if I had been born skinny and dark-skinned, but I have no doubt she would never hear the end of it from my aunts and grandmother.

Being a Buddhist, my mother was prohibited from eating beef, so she ate plenty of eggs instead. She didn't drink coffee either, so once again luck was on my side. I was born a fair and chubby little baby. Unfortunately, I was also as bald as an egg and have remained chubby to this day.

The use of foul language by my mother was avoided throughout her pregnancy lest I be cursed. She was told to avoid torturing, striking or killing any animal because anthropomorphic results might occur. This taboo was fairly easy for her to abide by because she never harmed animals even when she was not pregnant. However, she couldn't stand cockroaches and they were about the only things that she would have a hard time trying not to smash with her slippers. I assume she didn't kill any, for if she had struck one, I would have looked like a roach and behaved like one. Visits to places that had monkeys were strictly considered as taboo for fear that I would be born hairy and monkey-like.

My dad, on the other hand, broke certain rules when my mother was pregnant with me, or so I was told, which contributed to some flaws in my appearance. I was born with fistulas on the inside of my mouth and outer ears because he went fishing, and supposedly those were the hook marks. I do believe though that he probably did not gut the fish or slit its mouth to remove the hook, or I would have been born with a cleft-lip.

Frankly, I do thank my lucky stars that he wasn't a painter. As the child of a painter, I might have been born with patches of red marks plastered on my face. Worse still, if he had been a carpenter, I could very well have been born without limbs, and hammering nails was also thought to cause deformity in the foetus.

No shifting of furniture was allowed for the fear that my mother would suffer a miscarriage. In addition, my mother was cautioned not to step over ropes, especially ones used to tie up a cow or a goat, as this was believed to result in a difficult birth.

At last, the day of my birth arrived. 'Faster faster Ah Gaik, bring me a nail!' yelled my grandmother frantically as my mother started to feel labour pains.

My cousin Ah Gaik Chee rushed to look for a nail and hurriedly brought it over for my grandmother, who immediately inserted it into my mother's hair.

Seeing my mother's shocked expression, my Ah Mah patted her head and explained, 'The nail is to prevent evil spirits from entering your body when you are in labour.'

'Don't worry, I have taken care of everything to ensure a smooth delivery,' said my grandma as she continued to wipe the sweat off my mom's forehead with a cool towel.

'I have also prepared a glass of water with a key submerged in it just in case you experience any difficulties during delivery. You just have to drink the water and everything will be fine. The key will open your womb,' my grandma reassured my mother, who was now in great pain and probably quite terrified, this being her first pregnancy and childbirth.

One final decree from my grandmother before I made my appearance was that all the drawers and cabinet doors in the house were to be flung open to facilitate the delivery process. Considering the huge colonial bungalow we lived in, I suspect this proved to be quite a Herculean task.

# 3

# Ah Too, Ah Kau,
# Ah Goo—Pig, Dog, Cow

And so after half a dozen predictions and many dishes of taboos, on a Thursday evening, in the month of the Hungry Ghost (the seventh month in the Chinese calendar) I was born, a girl.

I am not sure how I feel about being brought into this world in the month where the gates of hell are opened for ghosts to wander around in the world of the living, to walk amongst normal people like you and I; but I guess I have no choice, so that's that.

For me it was a double whammy because apparently not just merely the month but also the date and time of my birth made my affinity with the spirit world and the dead much stronger. On the flip side, I do believe all things are destined, nothing happens by fluke. Even the family that I was born into has already been predetermined.

I was also born a year old, for the Chinese calculate their age from the date of conception and not the date of birth.

I was told, my dad wanted a son but I didn't believe it (although something did happen later on which made me think that perhaps the rumours were true. Will tell you about it later).

Anyway, at this point I truly did believe that my dad would have been happy with a son or a daughter.

I think it was his family that had hoped for a boy to carry on the Cheah name. Well, that is what I believe anyway, so I am not entirely sure if my birth was a joyous occasion. I remember my grandmother lamenting how unfair the Chinese family system was, as the female offspring were thought to be only 'temporary' family members. We would live with our families until we were married. As wives, we would then live with our husband's family and were deemed no longer part of our own family but the property of our husbands. In short, baby boys were more precious than baby girls, for only boys could carry on the family name.

Apart from being born a female, I also had the 'misfortune' of being born in the year of the Fire Horse. This combination was like a triple jeopardy. First, horses are regarded as outgoing, ambitious, rebellious and independent creatures, characteristics that would probably be prized in a Western society but are disliked and frowned upon in women in an Asian society. Women, especially wives, good wives with ideal female qualities are supposed to be submissive, quiet and dependent, not too ambitious or headstrong. Second, the fire element is regarded as voracious and powerful, making the Fire Horse woman uncontrollable, independent, freedom-loving and impossible to contain. No family could risk marrying their son to a woman with such undesirable qualities.

Whether they were sad or glad, happy or mad after all the trouble they had gone through, I had the audacity of being born a girl, they still had to choose a name for me. The choosing of a name was considered to be quite an important event. Most Chinese believe that a person's name plays an important role, especially in determining the person's destiny.

Grandma once explained to me that a typical Chinese name usually contains three characters. I would have a family name, a middle name which indicated my generation and a personal name. I was also told that just by looking at my middle name, I could trace back which generation I was born under and which 'rank' I was in relation to all my other relatives.

One fine day, when I was about ten years old, I confronted my mother and demanded to know why they had given me such an awful name.

Ma patiently replied, 'Lian ah, when a name is chosen it must have a favourable meaning.'

'So what about Mei Mei, what does her name Swee Ling mean? What is favourable about it?' I retorted. Mei Mei was what I called my baby sister, who was five years younger to me. As far as I knew, her name did not have any meaning.

I could see Ma was getting impatient, but she answered me anyway. 'That is not the only requirement for a name. It must sound pleasant when spoken, it must be harmonious with regard to yin and yang as well.'

I pressed on, still unable to fully comprehend. 'So Mei Mei's name, how is it in harmony with yin and yang?'

But Ma continued as if she had not heard my question. 'A name must also possess one of the five elements of metal, water, wood, earth, and fire, and last but not least, the name must reflect favourable mathematical calculations.'

When I was growing up, adults ignoring a child's questions was quite common. When asked about things which they were not sure of, or had no clue about, they would either ignore it or just ask you to be quiet and 'don't talk so much.'

'What do you mean, favourable mathematical calculations?' I asked, even though I knew I might not get an answer. At that point, my Cousin Charlie, who must have been eavesdropping nearby, interfered. Charlie was my Tua Kor's second son, and I called him Charlie KoKo ('older brother') since he was older than me. 'Aiyoh you are so stupid, Swee Lian, it means that if you add one plus one and it is two, in Hokkien 'tu' means pig; so the name is not favourable, you understand?'

Ma burst out laughing at the way Charlie explained in his 'know-it-all' manner. I am pretty sure his explanation was erroneous, but Ma did not confirm whether it was right either. She just continued to explain as if she did not hear my previous question at all.

'When a Chinese name is written, it must have a certain number of brush strokes. Each character's number of brush strokes corresponds to a certain element.'

'What do you mean "elements"?' I asked. This time Ma was not so patient. 'Stop asking questions, if you keep interrupting me, I won't be able to finish explaining.'

'Ok ok,' I relented, afraid my Ma would shoo me off to bed.

'Take for example, a two-stroke character is associated with wood, whereas the three- and four-stroke ones are fire.' After a brief pause she continued, 'Five- and six-strokes, I think signify earth, and nine and ten would be water.'

I had so many questions upon listening to her explanation but I bit my tongue and withheld them.

So when a question came from Cousin Charlie, I was relieved. It was the same question I had in mind. 'So do we add those strokes up for it to mean something?'

'Yes,' said Ma. 'The total number of strokes in a name could determine a person's fortune.'

'Waahhh,' both Charlie and I exclaimed simultaneously.

'How many strokes is considered good?' I burst out, unable to contain my question.

Ma's patience seemed to have been restored, as she replied calmly, 'If a name has twelve strokes in it, it can bespeak a life of illness and failure. And if it has eighty-one strokes in it, it presages prosperity and a happy fortune.'

In spite of my mother's long-winded explanation and claims that the Chinese supposedly did all of the above when choosing a name for a child, I had my own doubts that my father's family went through all that to choose mine. After all, I wasn't born a boy, so it really didn't affect them much whether I was successful in life or not. They did, however, follow the basic rules: my last name or surname was of course taken from my dad and his family, my middle name was the family's generational name, and the third one was a word that, when combined with the second, gave some semblance of meaning.

My name, Swee Lian, meant 'pretty lotus.' Why they would name me after a flower, I have no idea. It's not like I'm the delicate type of person, but of course they didn't know that at the time I was named. Why not a cool English name like Daphne or Melanie or Lindsay? I guess being Buddhist, my parents thought the lotus was a good name because it symbolizes purity of the body, speech and mind. The lotus rises above the muddy waters on long stalks, and perhaps that was their wish for me in life, to rise above attachment and desire. The drops of water that slides of the petals might also be symbolic of detachment. Regardless of the meaning, I really do not like my name.

Not only do the Chinese painstakingly calculate strokes to ensure success in life, but those of the Peranakan culture also believe that in case this calculation by some 'name-giving

Chinese guru' is wrong, the family has a right to mend it. For example, in my dad's case, they hardly ever called him by his official name, Jimmy Cheah Chye Huat. Instead, they called him by a nickname to prevent evil spirits from taking him away. After all, he was a boy, and by definition 'precious'.

When he was a child, my dad was nicknamed Tua Looi Bak, which means 'Big Eyes.' I guess if you think about it, big eyes on a dark-skinned puny baby actually conjures a very ugly picture. With a name like that, the evil spirit would surely pass over my dad and go on to find another baby whose ignorant parents had named something attractive like *Ming Mei*, 'Bright and Beautiful.'

Anyhow, I am just glad that my dad was nicknamed 'Big Eyes' and not something more horrible. Sometimes, before the umbilical cord was cut, a child was given a temporary or 'decoy' name in order to mislead the spirits of disease and illness. I've heard that some parents even go as far as calling their babies *Ah Too, Ah Kau, Ah Goo*, which means pig, dog or cow, in order to fool the Grim Reaper into believing that their babies are not human but rather piglets, puppies or calves—something not worthy of stealing away.

Others go as far as calling their babies by some other name intentionally to confuse and prevent ghosts and evil spirits from finding the baby and thus 'stealing' it away. For instance, if a child's real name was Lee Ming, he could be called Ming Ming, so that when the evil spirits came looking for Lee Ming, they would not find him. Calling their children by names such as '*Hitam*' (black), '*Busuk*' (smelly), '*Mata sepet*' (slanted eyes) or '*Botak*' (baldy), was also acceptable since it was supposedly an act of love—anything to persuade demons that their children were too unattractive to be their prey.

As you can see, nicknames were a thing with my family—everyone (or so it seemed to me) had one. Another reason a name might be changed was illness. The Baba-Nyonya culture believes that if the name given to the child is not suitable, the child will constantly fall ill.

To this day, I remember a cousin of mine who had to change his name because he was constantly ill when he was a baby. It was assumed that either his name was not suitable for his personality, or the number of strokes in his name (twelve) must have been unlucky or something.

Being people with a sense of humour, the Baba-Nyonyas give nicknames not only to babies and little children, but also to adults. This nickname habit turned out to be very useful, especially when we kids needed to address relatives at family gatherings. Just by physical appearance we knew which was which—the elder lady with all white hair was called Ee Ee Pek Mor (white-haired aunt), the man with the receding hairline was Botak Ah Khoo (bald uncle), and the fellow with a big head was Tua Thow Tneow (big head uncle).

When it comes to protecting a newborn, it was also a common practice for Baba-Nyonyas to give a baby boy a girl's name and make him wear a girl's dress in order to fool evil spirits into thinking that he was a girl and therefore, not worth stealing.

I am not sure if my dad was dressed up as a girl when he was a baby, though as I said, they did give him a nickname for protection.

In addition to changing names or giving nicknames, a child could also be given up for 'adoption' to a temple deity in hopes that the deity would protect them from the evil spirits that were making them prone to sickness. But don't worry, being 'adopted' by a deity does not mean you have to go live in a temple. It's just a symbolic gesture—at most, all you have to do is to pay respects to the deity one day each year during the deity's birthday and perhaps have a yellow string tied around your hand to identify you as one of the deity's 'stepchildren.'

My Da's adoption, however, was real, and it all happened even before he was born. No, it wasn't because of an unwed mother or poverty, which was the most common cause of giving up one's child back that time, but rather a promise between two best friends. Both families involved were equally wealthy. In fact, I think my dad's adopted family was perhaps even wealthier if I remember correctly, considering my grandmother's stories of riding around in her grand horse carriages, the numerous servants constantly serving them and the huge colonial-style houses they used to live in.

The Cheah family had two daughters and no son, whereas the Tan family already had two sons and two daughters; so a third son would have merely been a bonus for the Tans. As they were best friends and lived close to each other, I guess Mr Tan saw no harm in giving up his son to his best friend Mr Cheah so that the Cheah family name would live on. And so a promise was made: if the child born was to be a boy, he would be given to the Cheah family. I do not know the exact details of this 'transaction' other than what I had been told, but what seemed like an innocent and generous gesture between the two best friends turned out to be a very scary and traumatizing experience for my dad.

Initially they tried to cover up the adoption, but somehow the cat was let out of the bag by one of my father's cousins, Chung Hock Beng, who was not much older than my Da. Both boys and some other younger cousins were playing 'Police and Thief', a game where the group broke into two teams, one representing the thieves and the other, the police. Being the two eldest boys in the group, my Da and Ah Beng were naturally the leaders.

'Jimmy, do you want your team to be Police or Thief?' asked Hock Beng on a Sunday evening as they assembled in the front grassy compound of the bungalow.

'I prefer to be Police.'

'Ok sure, now everyone gather in a circle and put your right foot in. Come on, hurry up before the sun sets,' instructed Hock Beng impatiently.

All the five cousins gathered around and the assignment of teams started with Hock Beng reciting a Hokkien rhyme in a sing-song voice while touching each foot in the circle in a clockwise or anticlockwise manner.

*Chui Loh Chui Peng Peng*
*Choo Chui Chiak Pah Choe Lam Peng*
*Chui Loh Chui Chart Chart*
*Choo Chui Chiak Pah Choe Lam Chart*

(Chase on, chase the soldier
Whoever has eaten, will be the weak soldier
Chase on, chase the robber
Whoever has eaten, will be the weak robber)

The foot that his finger lands on when the last syllable is recited will determine which team that person is in.

The game went on for about twenty minutes before all the thieves were captured. My father jumped up and down pumping his fist into the air yelling 'winner, winner, winner' repeatedly.

Hock Beng scowled, for he had a bad temper and often had poor sportsmanship even when playing street games.

'It's ok lah, let you win,' he said slyly. 'After all, Ah Pek picked you from the *"sampah thang"*, you are a "trash bin" kid.'

'You take that back,' said my father angrily. 'That is a lie.'

'Oh okay, okay, yea that is a lie but this isn't, do you even know that you are an adopted child?' Hock Beng's words must have stabbed into my father really hard because his face turned all red and tears welled up in his eyes. My dad's quick temper got the best of him, and he punched Hock Beng in the face. A fight broke out between the two of them, and the commotion soon brought the adults out to separate the two. His eyes still red with tears, Da was made to apologize to Hock Beng, whose parents took him home in a huff.

That night Da asked Ah Kong about it and Ah Kong, as gently and lovingly as he could, told him the whole story of how he came to be a part of the Cheah family household.

In a way, the knowledge that he was adopted destroyed part of his childhood. Not in the way you might think—he wasn't abused or anything, in fact he was greatly loved by the Cheahs— but somehow knowing that he was 'given away' wounded my dad deeper than anyone of us ever realized, and his scars never healed. He always referred to himself as 'nobody's child,' and his deep insecurities affected many of his decisions in his life. However, one good thing did come out of his feelings of being 'unloved.' He, in turn, loved my ma, my sister and me with a fierce, devoted, and almost obsessive passion.

# 4

# Ugly Baby and Pomelo Leaves

Just as there were superstitions around my mother's pregnancy, there were also superstitions that governed proper behaviour when one is around newborn babies. I may have been cute as a baby but no one ever praised me, for it was believed that you should never praise a newborn baby lest it invite evil spirits and ghosts. It was, in fact, encouraged for everyone to refer to me with unfavourable terms and words.

'Oh, look at those big elephant ears, she's not a very pretty baby,' my Sar Ee, my mother's third sister, commented as she stroked my head affectionately, knowing full well that having wide and thick ears was a sign that the baby would live in prosperity.

'Oh, I see what you mean and her skin is not all that fair,' my Goh Ee, my mother's fifth sister, said while bouncing me on her lap and kissing my cheeks. 'I am sure it would be hard to find a husband for one so ugly.'

'Look at her navel, it's concave, how awful,' added Jee Ee, my mother's second sister, while she tickled me in the tummy. In case you are wondering, a concave navel is considered to be a sign of prosperity or that the baby would have a prosperous life.

An extruding one is less auspicious. So I guess when I was little, it was general consensus that I was an 'ugly' baby.

After giving birth to me, my mother was expected to observe a thirty-day period of confinement. During this period, she was not allowed to eat food that had 'cold' elements in it such as cabbage or green beans. Instead she had to eat food with 'warming' qualities such as steamed pork in black vinegar, chicken cooked in sesame oil and tons of ginger, pickled pig feet, and chicken cooked in red wine. Seafood was also a definite no because it was considered toxic.

Additionally, she was not allowed to go out, take cold showers or wash her hair during her confinement period.

Keeping warm was of paramount importance because after giving birth the body was considered weak and susceptible to possession by evil entities.

I figured keeping warm wasn't that difficult considering the weather in Malaysia—always a sweltering 98 degrees Fahrenheit and above.

But it must have been really difficult for my mother, not being able to take a shower or wash her hair. My mother was by nature a very clean person with very low tolerance for dirt.

Because this time was so crucial, special care was taken to protect not only the mother but also her child. It is believed that there is a Chinese ghost called the *See Loh Bun* of whom we have to be aware. This ghost takes the form of the head of a woman with intestines that trail behind it, dripping with blood. If her blood touches any human, severe sickness would follow. Her favourite victims are pregnant women, women who have

just given birth and young children. This ghost normally flies around at night and cackles to announce her presence.

To prevent attacks on the mother and child, sharp and prickly leaves are hung in houses or put on window sills and thorny bushes are placed around the perimeter of the house especially that are on stilts.

Apparently this would deter the ghost from coming near, as she is afraid that her entrails would get caught in the sharp leaves. It was a good thing that the flooring of our house was solid tiles and cement. If it had been floorboards, we would have had to scatter prickly pineapples under the house. Some pregnant women go as far as sleeping with scissors and knives under their pillow.

Since Malaysia is a multicultural country, we have to be aware not only of Chinese ghosts but also ghosts of other races. One such ghost was the infamous Pontianak, a Malay ghost. It is believed that the Pontianak is a woman who died during childbirth and has returned as a vengeful spirit. The Pontianak is known to turn up after the delivery of a baby to try and steal the newborn away because she hates to see other women have what she couldn't.

It is believed that during the daytime her spirit resides in the banana tree. You can also smell her when she is close by, for she gives off a nice floral scent similar to that of the plumeria flower, often followed by the stench of a decomposing body. The only way you could 'kill' the Pontianak was by ramming a nail into the nape of her neck. These spirits were just a few of the threats from which my family dutifully protected my mother.

Apart from taking care of my mother, it was also ensured that my baby spirit did not leave my body. It was crucial not to put white talcum powder on my face when I was sleeping, as my

wandering spirit might not recognize my face and would not be reunited with my body.

The business of ensuring my safety and my mother's well-being during her confinement period was taken very seriously by my dad's eldest sister, Tua Kor. She took charge of everything from my mother's meals to her resting times and my feeding. Tua Kor took charge of everything. She hated it when people disobeyed her and she ran a very tight ship as far as her household is concerned.

To me she seemed like a woman very much in control until later I learned of her dark secret and her deep disappointment in life, her destiny in which she had no control over.

During the Japanese occupation in Malaya, my Tua Kor was in her teens. She was a brilliant scholar and loved books. This much I know looking at her library full of books she received as prizes for being top of her class. She was also exceptional when it came to numbers. Complicated divisions, additions, multiplications thrilled her.

If not for the war, she would have most likely continued schooling and went to college. Unfortunately, due to circumstances, for her safety from the Japanese soldiers, she was hastily married off to a Chinese businessman, Lim Heng Soon, who would become my Tua Tneow (eldest uncle). A man her family had arranged, a man who had nothing in common with her, a man she most likely never would have chosen for herself. He did not have a fascination for literature like she did, he did not appreciate the things she did, she enjoyed Western movies and he enjoyed Chinese movies. They were as different as night and day, but were destined to be husband and wife till death do them apart.

I am not entirely sure if she was bitter about being forced into this marriage but I am sure she knew her family did it to protect her; it was after all for her own safety, and as for the man, he was a kind man, he grew to love her in his own way and I think, in the end she did learn to care for him too.

Tua Tneow was quite short for a Chinese too, shorter than Tua Kor, though as I mentioned before, my Tua Kor was a tall woman, so most men looked short compared to her. Standing at about 5 feet 2 inches, this uncle of mine had a funny little moustache that twisted up at the end. His bald head had about three or four hairs plastered down the middle and his eyes looked enormous behind his thick glasses, making him look rather like a goldfish. We secretly called him *kim hoo bak*, 'goldfish eyes,' behind his back. Truth be told, I believe he was also a smart man, although much of the time he kept to himself, often overshadowed by his wife.

Another aspect of my Tua Tneow that stood out was that in spite of his sometimes stern demeanour, he could also act like a *geena t'au*, a childish adult who taught us many games and often had interesting ideas like using the *chiok*, woven mat, as a sail for our makeshift boat and using cardboard boxes as our house to escape from the crocodiles.

Pretty hard not to love him. Tua Tneow, however, had this one habit we kids found really amusing. But it irritated Tua Kor beyond words. Tua Tneow liked to fart, and he would let out long and short farts anywhere and everywhere he liked. His favourite fart tactic was to ask us to pull one of his fingers. He would act like he was all in agony, begging us to quickly pull his finger. When we did he would then let out a long farting *pooooooottttttt* sound. We thought it was both hilarious and disgusting. Tua Kor, however, was not amused at all with this behaviour of his.

Her disapproval made it easy for us kids to tease her with this Hokkien rhyme. Especially when she was being stern with us and we wanted to get back at her.

*Ah Koh Bay Ark Nooi (Brother-in-law sells duck eggs)*
*Ah Soh Bay Tharm Phooi (Sister-in-law sells spittoons)*
*Ah Tneow Gau Pang Phooi (Mom's brother-in-law farts a lot)*
*Ah Khor Chuan Tua Khooi (Dad's sister sighs away her displeasure!)*

But it's all good, our family loves teasing each other, even my Ah Mah and Ah Kong love a good tease once in a while.

To me, teasing Tua Kor was the most fun. She suffered from something called '*Latah* Syndrome.' Whenever she was startled, she would jump and launch into a stream of profanities and perform a series of involuntary actions such as mimicking or dancing. It was most enjoyable to watch her.

One afternoon, as she was dozing off in her favourite *por ee*, a cloth armchair, I decided that it was the perfect time to pull this prank on her. Charlie and Geok Poh were nearby playing a game of Congkak.

'Hey watch this,' I whispered to them before I leapt out in front of Tua Kor and started clucking like a chicken, 'buck, buck, buck.'

Tua Kor was jolted awake, jumped out of her chair, ran around in circles flapping her arms and shrieking, 'Kok kok kay, kok kok kay, kok kok kay,' which means 'chicken, chicken, chicken.'

All of us burst out laughing as we watched her.

I liked teasing and annoying her, but I also loved my Tua Kor very much. She truly cared for me—when I was a little older, she took me to a temple and had me fitted with an orange talisman on my wrist to ensure my well-being. And so with her in charge, I started my new life well protected by my talisman and a single pomelo leaf placed under my mattress to ward off evil spirits.

# 5

# Red Eggs and Red Tortoise Cakes

At the full lunar month after my birth a small celebration *Muar Guay* was held to introduce me to friends, neighbours, and close relatives. This ceremony also marked the end of the confinement period for the baby's mother. For weeks, my aunts ran around like headless chickens preparing for this day. They made hundreds of *ang ku kueh,* small tortoise-shaped red cakes with a green bean filling.

If I had been born a boy, the cakes would have been round to symbolize the testicles of a male offspring. In this case, since I was born a girl, the cakes were 'flat' tortoise-shaped to symbolize, well I think you get the picture. In addition to the cakes, my aunts also painted hard-boiled eggs red. These red cakes and eggs were to be given to the guests to announce that a new infant has been born.

This *ang ku kueh* is served not only during a baby's one-month-birth celebration but also during other religious festivals like the Jade Emperor's birthday, *Cheng Beng* Festival and Chinese New Year.

My Jee Kor specialized in making this delicacy, so she was often appointed to oversee the making of these red tortoise cakes.

Besides placing great importance on food, we, Baba-Nyonyas, also love music and literature, often coming up with poems to depict life's daily comedies.

*Ah Mah Tng (Grandma Long)*
*Ah Mah Tay (Grandma Short)*
*Ah Mah Thau Jiak AngKuKueh (Grandma ate the red tortoise*
*cake without permission)*
*AngKuKueh Sio sio (Red tortoise cake was hot)*
*Jiak Liao Tiok Beh Pio (After eating will win the lottery)*

While eating this deep orange-red-coloured delicacy we would chant this to tease our grandma. This cake, though can be eaten cold, tastes best when it is hot. The texture of the skin is thin, soft and chewy and the moment you take a bite, you can taste the sweet slightly salty taste of the mung bean paste.

I remember one year there was a big birthday celebration for Ah Mah and we were all instructed to help out in the making of the ang ku kueh.

The preparation and cooking started early in the morning. Around 4 a.m. I could hear pots and pans banging in the kitchen. I rolled over, put a pillow over my head to drown out the noises and pretended to be asleep, but no sooner had I rolled over than I felt a tapping on my shoulder.

I continued pretending to be fast asleep, but my Ma knew me too well. All she had to do was walk away, saying, 'Ah Lian, see you down in the kitchen in five minutes.' Sleepily, I dragged myself out of bed, brushed my teeth, combed my hair, changed out of my pajamas and went downstairs.

When I arrived they had already mixed the rice flour into the boiling water. Jee Kor then took the peeled green beans, which had been soaked for three hours and steamed till soft, blended them till they were smooth and stir-fried them with sugar in a dry pan. After doing that, she left the filling to cool.

Both my older cousins Ah Gaik Chee and Ah Hwa Chee were mixing the glutinous rice flour with icing sugar and red colouring

together before adding it into Jee Kor's mixture of rice flour and boiling water. When they were done, the task of kneading the dough was given to Choo Choo Kor, my Tua Tneow's adopted sister (I will tell you more about her later on), who was the strongest of the lot. As she kneaded, she added oil little by little until the dough was smooth. Then she divided it into portions.

When all this was done, the kids could then step in and wrap the filling in the portions of dough.

We all enjoyed doing this because it was like playing with clay or play doh. After the mung bean was placed into the dough, we handed them back to Jee Kor and she would press each filled dough into an *angku* mould. After that she would gently slide out the tortoise-imprinted cake and put each one on a square piece of banana leaf.

The cakes were then arranged in a steamer and steamed for eight minutes on medium heat. I can still remember the sweet warm smells wafting through the house as the red tortoise cakes were being steamed.

Anyway (I digress), back to my one-month-old celebration. When the special day arrived, many guests came bearing gifts such as chicken essence for my mother, baby clothes wrapped in red paper and red packets containing jewellery for me. In return, a feast consisting of *nasi kunyit* (steamed glutinous turmeric rice) and chicken curry with potatoes were provided and of course, the red tortoise cakes.

'Oh, you didn't have to bring gifts, it's just a small get-together,' exclaimed my Tua Kor as she greeted each guest. Everyone knew that those comments were just for show, and a gift was expected from each guest.

Guests were encouraged to stroke my head so that it would become nicely rounded. Why, I don't really know. This also gave the guests an opportunity to examine my head and note that I have only one hair crown. It was thought that a baby with more than one hair crown would be mischievous and disobedient. Praise of any kind was still prohibited.

During this celebration, I also had an egg rolled over my head. Supposedly, the smoothness of the egg symbolized good looks and fertility. The day after the feast, whatever little hair I had on my head was shaved off. This ritual was observed because the baby's hair was regarded as 'interim' hair and its removal would facilitate the growth of permanent hair.

These superstitions followed me well into my childhood and adolescent years. They governed many of my actions or inactions and my parents, grandparents and aunts used these taboos regularly as a disciplinary tool. In those pre-Dr Spock days, I guess instilling fear into a child was the best and most effective parenting technique.

# 6

# Yellow Spirits and Cannibal Soup??

When I was growing up, my younger sister Swee Ling and I were not allowed to go out onto the playground during sunset because that was when the 'ghost people' came out to play. Most of these spirits, we were told, were benign. They were just like us mortals. They ate, drank, slept and played. I don't think they ever went to the bathroom though—I don't recall my aunts saying anything about ghosts needing to go.

There were, however, three kinds of ghosts that we had been warned about. I believe that almost all Malaysian kids had been told stories about them at some point in their lives while they were growing up.

The first ghost is the *Hantu Tek Tek* (ghost with pendulous breasts), who lives in big storm drains and wanders around during night-time. She kidnaps children playing outside their homes at night. If she catches you, she would force you to drink milk from one of her breasts, one side would be sweet milk and the other salty, if you chose the wrong one she would never let you go. Of course, the adults conveniently neglected to tell us which side was the 'right' side. That is why, according to my aunts, we were not allowed to play outside after dark or near storm drains.

Secondly, there are the 'yellow spirits' who linger during twilight. During this time, they are at the peak of their mischievousness. These spirits are the hardest to avoid because meeting them is often accidental. That is, you could bump into them as you were leaving the playground, heading for home. If a child falls sick after a particular sunset, it is believed that they are suffering from weakness of the spirit—the result of having encountered the 'yellow spirits.'

Playing hide-and-seek was also discouraged because of a hag that causes nightmares in children. While playing hide-and-seek, children may lose themselves in her prodigious breasts and be found days later dazed and foolish. Sometimes this vague dream-demon would take them to a thorn-brake and feed them earthworms and muddy water, which by her magic were transformed and made to look like delicious cakes.

Finally, there was the 'Orang Minyak' (oily man), the one we were most afraid of, because he specifically targets young unmarried girls. Also unlike the other two ghosts where we have a choice to stay away from, for instance to avoid the Hantu Tek Tek, we just have to stay away from drains and for the yellow spirits we just have to make sure we go home before twilight. As for the Orang Minyak, if he sets his sight on you and chooses to visit you, there is not much you can do because he is said to sneak into your bedroom and attack you while you are asleep.

There are, however, some things, we were told, might protect us from him. One of them was to wear a boy's sweaty clothes. I remember our ever-so-benevolent Cousin Charlie offering to sell us his T-shirts.

'Cheap, cheap, only one cent per tee; however, if you want one with extra sweat it will cost you two cents,' said Cousin Charlie to us one evening as we were getting ready for bed. When we wrinkled our noses in disgust, Charlie also offered to capture the Orang Minyak for us for a small fee.

'How will you do it? We heard that the Orang Minyak is very hard to capture because it is very difficult to see him in the dark and he is very slippery,' said Cousin Geok Poh skeptically.

'Don't worry, very easy only, I will hide behind the door with a piece of batik cloth, when he is standing there watching you sleep I will throw the cloth over him,' said Charlie with utmost confidence.

'Once he is weakened and his energy is sapped, one of you will have to bite his thumbs off, only then will he die.'

Geok Poh and I looked at each other; even without speaking, we both knew 'biting off thumbs' is out of the question.

'You crazy ah?' I scolded Charlie.

'Okay, okay,' Charlie raised his hand as if to placate us. 'No worries, you can also beat him with a branch from the petai plant. That will also kill him.'

I don't think we ever bought any of Charlie's T-shirts for protection or engaged any of the 'services' that he offered, though we did secretly scatter some banana heart petals and taro leaves around our bedroom.

Although we were bound by many taboos and superstitious warnings during our playtime, we were also allowed a lot of freedom. We could pretty much roam anywhere unsupervised as long as we make it home in time for dinner.

One day during the week of the *Cheng Beng* festival (Ancestors Day or Tomb Sweeping Day), Cousin Charlie, in one of his good moods, decided that once the adults left for the gravesite, he would take Mei Mei, Geok Poh and me to the waterfall behind our house.

'Waterfall?' Mei Mei's eyes were open wide.

'Ssshhhhh,' I cautioned her, 'don't make too much noise.'

'Yea, keep it down,' Geok Poh frowned. 'We certainly don't want anyone to find out about our plans.'

Cousin Charlie specifically warned us that we had to keep this adventure a secret because trekking into the forest to reach the waterfall during this *Cheng Beng* period was definitely a big 'NO'. If anyone in the family found out, we would all be in serious trouble.

Although it wasn't a very long hike in and the route was quite straightforward, we kids were never allowed to hike there by ourselves because the forest was considered a place that demands respect, and there were many rules surrounding it. Ah Mah used to tell us stories of spirits that lived in the jungle and how one needed to watch their behaviour when they were in the jungle or forest, lest they be punished by the spirits that reside there. It was also important to know the 'safety rules' of the forest, because we definitely wanted to avoid being cursed by the supernatural, and even more importantly, we did not want to inadvertently bring them home.

Going into the jungle or forest was much like visiting another person's house: whenever we visit someone else's house, we have to respect their rules and whatever customs they observe.

That morning all the adults were in such a frenzy preparing for the tomb visit that they hardly paid any attention to us, kids. We were shooed out of the kitchen whenever we entered, even if it was just to get a glass of water. The servants were always in a bad mood and grumbling about my *chay soo* fusspot grandmother, who had been hovering over them to ensure that all details governing the Cheng Beng ritual were correct to make sure that the spirits of our ancestors were appeased.

'Aiyoh, don't know how many times she need to remind me to pack the joss paper and the incense for burning,' I overheard one of the servants complaining to Choo Choo Kor, as I was passing by the kitchen door to go to the toilet. I stopped and hid behind the curtain to listen in.

'It's okay lah, this is a once-in-a-year thing,' said Choo Choo Kor calmly.

'It's a good thing they don't believe in burning paper gifts such as house, TV and cars,' Ah Hwa Chee, one of my cousins, said in a lighthearted manner. 'Otherwise we would have to lug those all up the hill.'

Ah Mah then yelled into the kitchen, 'Remember to pack the *kali kay* (curry chicken) and the *lobak* (five spice meat rolls), those are your *Tar Poh Chor*, great grandfather's favourite food.'

Not five minutes passed before Ah Mah poked her head in the kitchen again and instructed, 'Please pack the *kuihs* last because I don't want them to turn bad in this hot weather.'

'Okay, okay, will remember to do so,' replied Ah Gaik Chee as she turned to Ah Hwa Chee and said hurriedly, 'Remember to pack all the things we need to clean the tombstone. When we arrive, please start by removing all the weeds.'

Tua Kor finally came downstairs and reminded Choo Choo Kor to pack the wine and tea.

'Don't forget ah, it would be terrible to expect Ah Chor to eat all that food and then not having any beverage to wash it down. She then turned to Jee Kor who was behind her and said in a whisper, 'Nellie ah, please remind that *angmor ang*, English husband of yours, not to peep over other people's graves when he is there.'

Jee Kor nodded. 'I did remind him this morning and also to not simply say things or make comments on the deceased unless he wants to invite the spirits to latch on to him and follow him home.'

'It is very important not to step over someone else's grave and don't make too much noise. We don't want to disturb the spirits,' added Tua Kor. Jee Kor did not seem to be offended by all these reminders to keep her husband in check because she was well aware that Uncle Harry (being British and all) had a tendency to speak whatever was on his mind, and this was a 'dangerous' thing to do while one was in the graveyard.

I was still hiding behind the curtain, getting more and more impatient. Sweat was dripping onto my eyebrows and my left foot seemed to have fallen asleep. As I waited, my mind started to have conversations with itself. When are they going to leave? I wish they would leave soon, so we can sneak off to the waterfall.

I could see that the rest of the gang was getting restless too. Charlie kept throwing spitballs at Geok Poh, irritating her as she was trying to explain to Mei Mei the 'rules' of the forest.

'Have you heard of *sopok* and *pampuvan*?' she asked Mei Mei. My little sister shook her head.

'Well, *sopok* are like dwarves or gnomes and *pampuvan* are like leprechauns or fairies, these are forest spirits.'

'Geok Poh *chee-chee* should we be afraid of them?' Mei Mei asked, a little uncertain now.

'Well, they can be mischievous, often tricking or luring campers and hikers to follow them deep into the jungle. Once they follow these spirits in you, you will never be seen again. So listen up, it is very important that you remember what I am going to tell you now,' Cousin Geok Poh looked at my sister with all the seriousness that she could muster.

'This is no joke. If you see a termite mound, you have to be very respectful of it and not disturb it in any way. These mounds are supposedly the abode of the forest spirits and you should take extra care not to offend them. If you need to pee, please "ask for permission" to avoid being cursed and also to pay respects to the Datuk Kong, who is the guardian spirit of the jungle. Make sure you don't pick any items from the forest and bring it home. Can you remember all that?'

Mei Mei nodded silently, her eyes wide open. 'What else?'

'Make sure you don't sit on any rock formations. Sometimes malevolent spirits rest there. I think that's it,' Geok Poh concluded, glad that she had done her duty and 'educated' Mei Mei.

Finally, the adults were ready to leave for the graveyard. Each one of them except Ah Mah carried a basket filled with all the things that were needed for the ritual. Before leaving, Tua Kor turned to her son Charlie and instructed him, 'Make sure you don't get into any mischief and take care of your little cousins.'

As we waved the cars goodbye, we hurriedly snuck out through the backdoor. The three of us gathered around Charlie waiting for him to lead us.

'Swee Lian, when we are in the forest I will call you *Kacang Panjang*, long bean. Geok Poh, since you already have a nickname *Hor Chio Liap*, peppercorn, I will just call you that and Mei Mei, I will call you *Gu Leng Knia*, milk kid because you love to drink milk.' Charlie assigned us each a nickname because in the forest we should never yell out to each other using our real names, lest a spirit should hear it and trap us in their deadly realm.

'What should we call you?' I asked Charlie.

'Hmm let me see,' he pretended to ponder before replying, 'All of you can address me as *Tua Thaukeh*, Big Boss.' Geok Poh and I rolled our eyes but there was no time to argue. The sooner we left, the earlier we'd get there, and the more time we'd have to play.

Getting there was not a problem. The sun shone brightly and we just had to follow the stream all the way up. We arrived at the waterfall, quickly took off our shoes and started wading in the waters, it was so cool and refreshing. We played till around lunch time before we stopped to have the egg sandwiches we brought along and drank the packets of Yeo's chrysanthemum tea. After lunch, we played for another hour or so before Charlie said we would be leaving in about five minutes. We dried our feet in a small patch of leaves near the falls and put our shoes back on, carefully packing up all of the trash before setting out for home.

We walked for about fifteen minutes following the stream. The same route we took going to the waterfall but somehow we ended up walking in circles. We seemed to pass by the same banana tree a couple of times, always coming to a dead end, regardless of which way we turned.

Charlie was beginning to sense that something was not right. Somehow our vision must have been 'blocked' by spirits. Being the oldest, he immediately took charge, he pointed to Mei Mei and said, 'Quick, you have to squat down and pee.'

Mei Mei and I were puzzled. 'Why?' I asked, confused. 'Why does she have to pee now?'

'Yea, why?' asked Mei Mei, about to burst into tears.

'That's the only way to break the spell,' insisted Cousin Charlie. 'Do you or do you not want to go home?'

'But I don't need to go now,' Mei Mei stomped her foot stubbornly.

Charlie shrugged his shoulders. 'Up to you. It's either you'—he pointed at Mei Mei—'or you,' he said, pointing directly at me.

Looking at my sister's terrified face, I decided that it was easier for me to just do it than wasting my precious time trying to convince Mei Mei.

I chose a small bush, went behind it and was just about to slide my underwear down, when Cousin Charlie yelled out 'Remember to *pai pai*, ask the spirits' permission before you pee,' he reminded me.

I quickly clasped my hands together in a prayer motion and prayed to my left, to my right, in front and behind while softly mumbling, 'Please allow me to pee here, I don't mean to trespass, please forgive me if I did.'

After the deed was done, we resumed walking. Periodically, Cousin Charlie would turn around and remind us, 'If you smell anything fragrant or smelly please do not say anything.'

Geok Poh, Mei Mei, and I nodded silently.

'Oh and remember if you hear someone calling your name, DO NOT, and I repeat DO NOT turn around. Keep walking straight.' Cousin Charlie looked at us dead serious as he said this. Somehow, after walking for about another fifteen minutes or so, we found our way out.

Heaving sighs of relief, upon arriving home, all four of us made a beeline for the bathroom. No, it wasn't to pee but rather to wash our hands and feet. Cousin Charlie was the first to grab a bucket. He started scooping water from the big pottery water urn which had Chinese dragon designs on it and splashed them onto his feet. While splashing, he moved his feet back and forth vigorously rubbing the soles against the cement floor. After he was done he handed the plastic bucket to me. 'Nah I am done, please make sure you wash up well.'

I nodded as I took the plastic bucket from him. Peering into the urn I could see that there was a variety of colourful flowers floating in it. That was a good sign, for it meant that this water had already been prepped for cleansing and warding off evil spirits.

In the background I could hear Ah Mah's voice asking if everyone that had participated in the Cheng Beng ritual had already *mandi bunga,* taken their floral bath, to remove any evil element that could have followed them home.

Not wanting the adults to find out that we had made our secret excursion to the waterfall, I hurriedly motioned to the two girls, 'Hurry up, hurry up, Mei Mei and Geok Poh, why don't the three of us stand in a circle, put our feet close together. That way we can all wash our hands and feet together.'

The two of them immediately scooted in close, and I proceeded to scoop up water in the pail and splashed it in the centre of our circle so that our hands and feet were splashed simultaneously.

This washing of hands and feet after playing outside was not an unusual practice in our household. It is believed that if you do not wash your hands and feet after playing outside, you are inviting those spirits that may have followed you home into your house with you. Especially today after our experience of not being able to find our way home, we all knew we needed to wash up to make sure that we got rid of any 'trail' or 'scent' that might attract the attention of any lingering malevolent spirits.

After that incident, Geok Poh, Mei Mei and I stayed away and did not go back to the waterfall area for quite a while.

That night Tua Kor, the storyteller of the family, oblivious that we had disobeyed her orders and snuck out to the waterfall, decided that she would reward us for our good behaviour by telling us a story.

'Come, come, everyone, all the *geena kong*,' she ushered us children into the living room. 'Since all of you are so *kwai* today, so good and obedient, I will tell you all a story tonight.'

'What story, Tua Kor?' asked Mei Mei.

'Since it is *Cheng Beng*, I will tell you about the origin of this festival.'

All of us sat up straight and leaned forward, as we always loved Tua Kor's stories.

'Once upon a time after a civil war in China, there lived a prince called Chong Er who was forced to exile to the mountains.'

But before Tua Kor could continue, she was interrupted by Jee Kor.

'Wasn't it a guy named Duke Wen of Jin?'

'Hmmm,' Tua Kor pondered for a while. 'I am not sure, could it be the same guy, just different names?'

Jee Kor shrugged her shoulders, indicating that she didn't know either.

'Anyway, this prince was exiled because his concubine framed him for the rebellion. Apparently when he was banished into the mountains, his loyal minister, Jie Zitui followed him.'

'After a while they ran out of food.'

We held our breath for a second wondering what would happen, would the Prince and his loyal minister both starve to death?

'So what happened, did they both die?' asked Charlie impatiently.

'Actually no, they did not die because the loyal minister managed to make some soup for his prince. The prince was so grateful, he drank the soup to the very last drop and exclaimed to his minister how wonderfully delicious it was. He then asked his minister where he got the meat from to make such a delicious soup.'

Suddenly I felt a little uneasy, but did not dare to interrupt.

'Well, what happened was, the minister had sliced off a part of his thigh to make the soup for the prince,' said Tua Kor, her lips appeared tight as if she was trying to keep herself from laughing upon seeing our looks of horror.

'Ewwwwww,' Geok Poh exclaimed loudly.

'Yucks!!' I said and screwed up my face in disgust.

'Okay, okay, do you want me to continue or not?' asked Tua Kor.

'Yes!!' all of us replied simultaneously.

'Soon their hardship was over because the evil concubine died and the prince returned to the kingdom and became king.'

'Tua Chee, you forgot about the part where the prince, after drinking the thigh soup, promised to reward the minister for his loyalty,' Jee Kor chipped in to remind Tua Kor of that part of the story.

'Yes, yes, he promised his minister that. However, when they returned to the kingdom the prince, who is now the king, had completely forgotten his promise. Naturally the minister was upset. One night he decided to take his mother with him and leave for the mountains.'

'The king must have been very upset when he can't find the minister,' I said with certainty.

'You are right, the king was upset, and he had also realized that he had forgotten all about his promise to Jie.' Tua Kor continued.

'So what did he do?' asked Mei Mei.

'Well someone suggested to the king that perhaps he should burn the mountains to smoke the minister and his mother out.'

'What a stupid idea,' said Charlie, rolling his eyes.

'Yes, actually it was indeed a stupid thing to do because in doing so he had accidentally also burned his minister and his minister's mother. Full of remorse, he ordered his subjects to hold a memorial ceremony of Jie Zitui, and that ceremony is what we know today as *Cheng Beng*.'

We were all silent for a while, slowly digesting what we had just heard. I think basically it wasn't the story any of us had expected. I finally voiced what was in our minds.

'This story is so unexpected, I always thought *Cheng Beng* had to do with just honouring our ancestors. Who knew it all started with cannibal soup!'

'Oh well, it is what it is, now it's time for all of you to go to bed.' Tua Kor stood up and gestured for us to go to sleep.

As we stood up, one of the servants, Ah Hoon Cheh, entered carrying a tray with cups of piping hot Milo (our favourite chocolate beverage) and a plate of crispy, light and creamy Jacob's Crackers that were perfect for dipping. We drank up all the hot chocolate and polished off the entire plate of crackers. Then we brushed our teeth and went to bed happily.

Together with Cousin Charlie we went on many more secret adventures. Charlie was like a big brother to us; he protected us, but he also got us into quite a lot of trouble at times. Nevertheless, it was fun to have him around sometimes. But mostly, we three girls hung out: myself, Mei Mei, and Geok Poh.

I remember the first time, Geok Poh told us that she had 'special' eyes.

'Special eyes? What do you mean special eyes?' I remember asking her.

'Do you mean your eyes can do magic tricks?' said Mei Mei innocently.

'No, dummies,' said Geok Poh. 'My eyes are special, kinda like a "third eye" that can see things, you know, like ghosts and stuff.'

My sister and I held our breath and looked at each other tentatively, not sure what to make of this information. Our aunts had always told us that there were people out there who could see ghosts, but what were the odds that our cousin was one of them?

We were impressed yet a little scared. From that day on we made sure we were especially nice to her and included her in all our games.

Geok Poh was by nature a very sensitive girl and often took offense easily. If I said that my pretend cakes were delicious, it meant that hers were horrible-tasting. If I drew a pretty dress for my paper doll, it meant that her paper doll's pantsuit was ugly. Once I remember making her angry, though I can't remember exactly what I did. I don't even know at which point I made her angry because Geok Poh had a habit of not demonstrating her anger at the precise moment when someone made her mad.

Anyway, oblivious to the fact that I had made Geok Poh angry, I continued playing with her. Suddenly, she stopped whatever she was doing and looked straight at me. She had no expression on her face except her beady eyes moved slightly to the right as if looking at something behind me.

'Remember, my special eyes?' she whispered, staring stonily in my direction.

A shiver ran up and down my spine. I began to cry.

'Geok Po...ooh,' I choked out as I tried to swallow the lump in my throat, 'what is it?' I pleaded with tears streaming down my face.

Geok Poh remained stubbornly silent. She stood there for what seemed like an eternity to me. Slowly a smile played over her curled lips and she said, 'Nothing,' before taking off like a jackrabbit spooked by the scent of a dog. Guess that was her way of punishing me for offending her.

She did that so often that we made Geok Poh our official 'ghost-sighting' informer. She was very pleased at being given such an important role. It suited us fine, for we were then free to play until just before the sunset, relying on Geok Poh's 'special'

eyes to tell us when it was the 'ghost people's' turn to use the swings.

Mei Mei and I trusted Geok Poh and her special 'third' eye without ever questioning it. It wasn't until I was about nine years old when an incident happened, which made me think that perhaps I too might have the ability to see spirits.

One evening as I just got back from school, my father seemed unusually excited and was hurrying me through my homework and chores.

'Hurry up Swee Lian, we have to be there before 9p.m., today is a special day,' said my Da as he packed two bottles of water and a face towel into a plastic bag.

You see, my father was an avid believer of the occult and I was often dragged to temples to observe these rituals, seances and exorcisms. He was also appointed 'helper' to this medium whom I called 'Uncle Lim'.

'But Da, I don't want to go, I have a lot of homework and I am tired.'

'Tired, thaaaayert, yesterday when you got home from school, you went straight out to the playground and met up with your friends. Why no tired then?' my dad mumbled loud enough for me to hear him.

'Well, today we had to stay back for sports practice for Sports Day. Please can I not go?' I tried to explain one more time and for effect, I slumped my body on the sofa as if from exhaustion.

'I can't leave you alone at home, your Ma is still visiting her sisters in Tumpat.'

With that I decided to keep quiet and not argue anymore. There was no way he was going to leave me alone at home, no matter what I said.

That night turned out to be one of the nights I would remember for the rest of my life.

A young teenage boy was brought in by his relatives, who claimed he was acting strange. I remember peeking out from behind the yellow and red silk curtain, which separated the altar hall and our living quarters. It was about 8.30p.m. when they brought him in. The boy seemed normal except his head was bowed low, his long hair covering his eyes, and he shuffled like an old man. He obediently allowed them to lead him to one of the long line of plastic red chairs that was arranged on the sides of the walls.

He sat there quietly until the medium entered the hall and then all of a sudden, he stood up and started to prance restlessly and chant in a high-pitched tone, in a language that was foreign to me. His tongue started flicking like a snake and his eyes turned up, only showing the whites.

The medium seemed unperturbed and continued to don his shabby brown cotton garment, which he always wore before going into a trance. He then sat down and while holding some joss sticks in one hand, his body started to sway, his arms waving in a rhythmic fashion and he shook his head left and right while chanting. Suddenly he stood up with a fierce look on his face. The medium's face seemed to have gotten darker and his eyebrows seemed thicker, and his mouth turned up in a sneer.

He walked over to the still prancing teenage boy and threw some holy water at him. The demonic dancing figure screeched as the holy water touched its skin and he tried to sidestep away. The medium continued chanting.

'Hold the boy down, hurry hold him down, he is at his weakest now!' he instructed his assistants as he thrust his joss sticks menacingly towards the figure. The boy struggled violently, his mouth open wide, drool trickling from the sides down his chin as slurred eerie ululations escaped his lips.

'*Namo Kwan Say Im Phor Sat, Namo Kwan Say Im Phor Sat,*' I chanted silently in my heart, calling desperately for the Goddess Of Mercy to protect me. I was quite traumatized by what I had observed.

'Leave this boy alone,' commanded the medium as he hovered over the teenage boy. 'Let him go or there will be consequences, you have no right to inhabit his boy, he does not belong to you,' the medium continued before resuming his chant.

Suddenly the boy stopped struggling and his limp body started to curl up in a heap on the floor. As I started to sigh with relief, I saw a small dark creature that crawled on all fours climbing out of the boy's body. Before disappearing into the dark corner of the ceiling, the creature slowly turned, as it was crawling away, its white unseeing eyes seemed to be looking straight at me. For a second our eyes locked and I caught a glimpse of the upturned corners of its mouth, teeth gleaming, almost like it was smiling at me.

To this day I am not exactly sure what it was that I saw. Perhaps it was just the lighting or my imagination playing tricks on me. Also I was very tired that night. Perhaps I might have dozed off briefly and dreamt it all. I never told my parents or anyone of this incident. I kept quiet and continued to let Cousin Geok Poh be the official 'ghost-sighting' informer. Besides, I didn't want to risk upsetting her by claiming that I too could see spirits, thus making her less special.

In my eyes, Geok Poh was truly gifted and I believed that she truly did know a lot when it came to the supernatural world.

Geok Poh also taught us that if we wanted to see ghosts and the spirit world, we should smear a dog's eye-gunk on our eyes, bend down and look between our legs, and we would have the ability to see ghosts.

'Dogs have the ability to see supernatural beings such as ghosts and wandering spirits,' she explained in her matter-of-fact voice, 'and everyone knows that when you hear a dog howling, it means it's seeing a spirit.'

We were quick to believe Geok Poh's claim because we had seen with our very own eyes a medium smearing the eye-gunk on his eyes in order to see the supernatural world so that he could perform an exorcism.

However, we also remembered overhearing that if the ordinary person were to do the same, he or she might die from the shock of seeing the afterlife. So we never dared.

Being restricted by many more taboos and superstitions was a normal part of my growing up.

There was nothing weird about Tua Kor yelling out, 'Stay away from the bushes and drains when you are playing, that's where the *tok kehs*, geckos like to hide especially when the weather is hot.'

'Okay, okay, we know, we know, if we get bitten by a *tok keh* at noon we would die' one of us would yell back as we have heard this warning countless times.

Even today I can't think of even one aspect of my life that was not governed by taboos of some kind. Even during mealtimes, there were many dos and don'ts. Before sitting down for dinner (or any meal, for that matter), the younger ones in the family had to personally invite all those that were older than them to *chiak* (eat). Since I lived with so many relatives, it took a good five whole minutes to call everyone to eat, starting from Ah Kong and Ah Mah, the oldest in the family, down to my aunts, uncles and older cousins.

'Ah Kong *chiak*, Ah Mah *chiak*, Da *chiak*, Ma *chiak*, Tua Tneow (eldest uncle) *chiak*, Tua Kor (eldest aunt) *chiak*, Jee Tneow (second uncle) *chiak*, Jee Kor *chiak*, Charlie KoKo (elder boy cousin) *chiak*, Ah Gaik Chee-chee (elder girl cousin) *chiak . . .*' and so on and so forth.

By the time I was done 'calling' everyone I was famished. During one of those meal times, I think it was dinner, after having called everyone to eat, I plopped down onto the closest chair, hastily picked up a fork and reached out to help myself to a piece of *inche kayBin* (Nyonya deep fried chicken) drumstick which was in a dish across the table. At the same time my dad had reached out to scoop some *jiu hu char* (stir-fried jicama with sliced shiitake mushrooms and shredded cuttlefish) from the dish across from me. Or was he aiming for his favourite dish *kio masak belanda,* a simple but tasty dish of eggplant and prawns cooked in shrimp paste and coconut milk sauce? Occasionally there would be pieces of cashew nuts sprinkled on top of it.

I can't recall exactly which dish he was reaching out for but our hands crossed and he boomed at me, 'Swee Lian!!' I was startled and quickly withdrew my hand.

'How many times do I have to tell you, never allow your hands to cross someone else's hand during meal time.' He looked really upset as he scolded me, but held back from making a scene.

Crossing hands during mealtimes was frowned upon as this might cause a quarrel between the two people who crossed hands. This rule was one that my father religiously observed. I remember being yelled at countless times for stretching my hands across his to get to a dish. In hindsight, I think my father was more upset about the fact that my hands were blocking his view of the food he was about to take (thus delaying its journey to his mouth), rather than actually believing in this taboo. Plus, with my hands in the way, he probably couldn't see what he was picking up. Anyway, regardless of what I thought, I still obeyed the taboo and tried to abide by it.

Another one of the 'don'ts' that I found especially difficult to follow was the *'No changing seats during meal time'* rule.

'Swee Lian, how many times do I have to tell you, once you have chosen a seat at the dinner table you are not allowed to change seats?' my mom scolded me as I was squirming uneasily. I had just asked my cousin Geok Poh to switch seats with me.

'But why? Why can't I change seats, I hate sitting next to the toilet.'

'Well you should have thought of that before you sat down.'

'Please, please let me change this once.' I begged my mother. Instead of replying to me, she chose to change the subject by asking if I wanted some fish.

'No thanks,' I replied curtly. Mei Mei then said she wanted some.

Ma stood up to scoop some fish for her.

'Ah Suan, there is no more meat left on this side of the fish, take bones off, just take the bones off and you can scoop the bottom part of the fish for Mei Mei, there is less bones there too,' suggested my Tua Kor, indirectly reminding my mom to not flip the whole fish.

Geok Poh, who had been silently stuffing her face, suddenly decided to ask 'Why can't we just flip the fish? Isn't it easier than going through the trouble of picking off the bones?'

It was an innocent question, a question I would have asked if she had not. It made sense to me too, to just flip the fish.

The elders at the table rolled their eyes at her question and then looked at Jee Kor since she was Geok Poh's mother. It was her responsibility to educate her child.

'To turn over a whole fish is considered bad luck and also bad manners,' Jee Kor replied, 'that's why we don't do it. It is considered similar to turning over a fishing boat and that could bring misfortune to our family.'

When she was done explaining I decided to try my luck again at changing seats, but once again my request was denied.

'No, if you do that, it would mean that you would marry multiple times. Depending on the number of times you switched seats. Do you want that to happen?' Ma asked me in a stern voice.

Somehow, even at that young age, it was drilled into me that marrying more than once was not a desirable thing. It meant that either my first husband would die and therefore I had to remarry or that my first husband would divorce me—an even worse fate in the eyes of society at that time. In which case it would make me an outcast.

Bearing that in mind, I stopped asking if I could change seats. From then on, I would always sit in the same chair for every meal until I was done eating.

If you thought I was the only one who got into trouble during meal times you would be mistaken. My Cousin Charlie frequently got scoldings from his mom and my grandma too. Charlie, being a growing boy, often piled heaps of food upon his plate at mealtimes.

Whenever he did that, Ah Mah would glance at Tua Kor to see if she was going to give her son an earful.

'Charlie,' warned Tua Kor, 'remember what I told you before, stop doing that.' Charlie would glance at Tua Kor in a cheeky manner and hurriedly take a huge final scoop before putting the ladle down.

Apparently food is heaped only when serving to the deceased. Doing so was frowned upon during our daily meals.

Singing or humming was also prohibited during meal times. If we were caught doing so, we were told that we would be doomed to marry an old man (or an old woman, in the case of little boys).

It was an unwritten rule that plates should be cleaned to the very last morsel. If we left so much as one grain of rice on the plate that would mean a pimple would appear on our face the very next day. The more rice left on the plate the more pimples on our face. Polishing food off our places had never been a problem for me growing up in a Peranakan family, for we always had delicious food. Chewing food while lying down was one of the things I never did as well, lest I become a snake!

Oh, while we are on the subject of snakes, talking about snakes was also prohibited in our household. It was not an easy topic to avoid; since our neighbours started rearing chickens, we had been finding snakes hiding in various places in our home. We had to be extra careful when going to the toilet because snakes often slept under the toilet bowl, where it was cooler. On a couple of occasions, I also found snakes inside my folded blanket.

'Ma, Ma, I think there is a ss . . .' I would start to say, but my Ma immediately cut me short before I could say the 'S' word. According to Ma, if we said the 'S' word, it was like inviting it into our home to stay, so we had to refer to the snake as 'Mr Long.' We were also cautioned against trying to kill it. If we did, we would have to make sure that it was truly dead, or else it would come back for revenge.

'If you just injure it and let it escape, it will come back at night and bite you,' my Ah Mah would warn us.

Other taboos included not clipping one's fingernails or toenails during the night. This act was absolutely forbidden because it was believed to bring bad luck, perhaps causing a visit from the dead.

'Lian, Lian, where are you?' I heard my mother calling out for me one afternoon. I was hiding behind the hibiscus bush at the back of our house cutting my toenails.

As she called out more urgently, I had no choice but to respond, 'Yes Ma, I am behind the bush.'

'What are you doing there?' asked my Ma.

'Well, you told me that I had to make sure my nail clippings are disposed off secretly so that no one can find them and use them to cast a spell or curse on me, that's why I am hiding,' I explained to my mom.

'Ah good girl! You remembered,' Ma praised me.

'Why did you call me?' I asked my Ma, 'do you need help with anything?'

'Oh, no, no, I don't need help with anything. It's just that your Tua Kor was going to take all the kids out for a car ride tonight after dinner,' Ma replied, 'I just came out to see if you wanted to go too.'

'Yes, yes,' I replied excitedly as I hurriedly swept my nail clippings into a newspaper and folded it up.

That night after dinner as we piled into the car, we were laughing and singing happily. We had the windows rolled down to feel the fresh air caressing our faces as we looked up at the moon following us.

'Remember ah, do not point at the moon or your ears could get cut,' Tua Kor turned around to make sure none of us did that.

I believe this taboo because I've tried it and my ears did get cut. I can't explain exactly how but each time I point at the moon, a cut would mysteriously appear behind my ear the next morning.

What I've described above are only some of the daily taboos that we had to observe. For women, there are many more 'rules' that we have to follow when we have our monthly periods.

When my period came, my aunt warned me that if I should ever wash my hair on the first day of my period, I would get dark ugly circles under my eyes. I should also never ever borrow a sanitary pad from another person because that would cause the other person to have bad luck. If I ever did borrow one, I should pay the person 1 penny. Used pads should also be thrown away properly lest a ghost should find it.

Funny, as a child and even as a teenager, I never questioned the validity of these claims. I just assumed that since they were told to me by authority figures such as my aunts, mother, older cousins and both grandmothers, they must be true. Besides, these taboos sounded as normal as 'look both ways before crossing the street' or 'don't talk to strangers' to us.

In fact till this day, strangely I continued to follow these taboos. I still do not wash my hair on the first day of my period. Perhaps not so much out of the fear of getting dark circles under my eyes but mainly because I was usually in too much pain to even want to wash my hair. And I am often curled up, wrapped in my blanket like a cocoon with my hot water bottle. As for taking a penny each time someone asks me for a sanitary pad, I still do it.

In view of all the strange superstitions that surround me, one would naturally assume that my most horrifying memories might be meeting with a ghost, falling sick after a yellow sunset or being caught by the fat drain lady. But that wasn't the case. It wasn't ghosts or evil spirits that left me scarred.

# 7

# Turtles Don't Die Right Away

One morning, Choo Choo Kor came home all worked up from what I thought was her usual trip to the wet market. She was carrying two big rattan baskets filled with what looked like the usual weekly supply of fresh foods: eggs, chicken, fish, pork ribs, shrimp, and a variety of Chinese greens.

'Ah Lian, Ah Lian, *lai, lai,* come, come, I'll show you something,' she called to me in Hokkien, beckoning me to come closer.

'Look, look,' she said, lifting the cover and pointing into one of her rattan baskets.

'What?' I asked as I squatted next to her, peeping into the basket with curiosity. At first I saw nothing but a bunch of watercress leaves. Suddenly the leaves moved, and out poked a turtle's long wrinkled neck, stretching far out of its shell as if curious to see me too.

'Careful, Ah Lian,' cautioned Choo Choo Kor, 'it can bite you.'

I was fascinated. The turtle looked so cute. Being a child, I did what every child did upon finding an interesting specimen. I looked around for a stick to poke it with. Having found one, I started poking one end of it at the turtle's head.

'Ah Lian, ah don't do that,' said Choo Choo Kor as she tried to pat my hand away. I ignored her feeble attempts to stop me. After all, this flat-footed woman wasn't even my real aunt. As I mentioned earlier, she was Tua Tneow's adopted sister—when his parents died, he inherited many things, and Choo Choo Kor was one of those 'things.' She became his 'property,' and that was how she came to live with us.

Choo Choo Kor was a Chinese spinster, often looked down upon and treated like a second-class citizen compared to her married peers. In our family, this short, stout woman with turnip-shaped legs and thinning vermicelli-white hair was regarded more like a servant than a family member.

The story we were all told was that at a young age of about thirteen, Choo Choo Kor was sold to the Lim family. During those times, rich families would buy young girls from poor families to serve as servants under the pretext of adoption. This was a much more economical way to procure a servant for life. You paid a one-time fee of about $100–$200 (which was a considerable amount in those days) to her biological family and you got someone who would serve you for your lifetime and even after you'd passed on, would continue to serve your children.

Additionally, families who 'adopted', were viewed as compassionate. However, if you hired a servant, you had to pay her monthly wages besides food and lodging. Furthermore, they were free to quit at any time and would not hesitate to do so if you mistreated them.

Sometimes the more resourceful of these 'adopted' girls managed to escape by finding themselves a husband, often a fishmonger, butcher or vegetable vendor at the marketplace they frequented daily to buy groceries for the family. Unfortunately, this shabby-looking aunt of mine was not one of these resourceful girls (or so I thought, not knowing the actual reason why she was never interested in finding a husband) for behind her broad brown face and shovel-nose lay a hillbilly personality. This simpleton had only one dream, and that was to go back to China and die. Even this dream was frequently stomped on and ridiculed by various members in the family, especially my grandma.

'If Heng Soon's family hadn't been so kind to adopt you, you would have been sold to prostitution long ago,' Grandma would say. 'Huh, you think China is so good, try going back. Who will take you? You can't even go to the corner sundry shop without getting lost!'

The outcome of these scenes between my Ah Mah and Choo Choo Kor was always the same. They invariably ended with Choo Choo Kor professing her 'mistake,' her 'stupidity,' and begging my grandmother, the matriarch of the family, to allow her to stay.

So when it came to household status, I knew that I, being the granddaughter of the Cheah family, held a much higher status than an adopted aunt. Since she lacked the power to control what I did, most of the time I ignored her admonitions.

'Ai-yah, Ah Lian, don't do that,' repeated my Choo Choo Kor as I continued probing the turtle with my stick. 'Listen to me, you naughty girl.'

When the stick touched the turtle's neck, it whipped his head around, opened its mouth wide and *snap!* The turtle held on to my stick with such tenacity that I had trouble wrestling it away. Finally, I grew tired of this game and left the turtle alone.

Every day for the next two weeks, I took care of the turtle with the help of Choo Choo Kor. I even named it 'Mi Koo,' after the red-skinned steamed Tortoise buns that were usually made for ancestral worship or offerings during the Nine Emperor Gods Festival.

I fed Mi Koo various foods such as carrot sticks, mealy apples and watercress leaves, and watched him swim in his little makeshift pond. Choo Choo Kor and I found a big old round aluminum tub like the ones used for washing clothes, and decided that it would make a suitable habitat for Mi Koo.

Each morning, after my breakfast, I would visit Mi Koo. When Mi Koo heard me coming, he would poke his head out of his shell and twist it this way and that as if looking for me.

I would pretend that he was my pet dog and even tried to take him for a walk, except that I had a hard time putting a rope around his neck. Finally, I tied it around his body and managed to drag him around the courtyard.

One morning when I went out to look for Mi Koo, he was gone. I looked everywhere for him. First I looked under his watercress leaves thinking that he might be hiding there. Then

I looked in the doghouse. Maybe he had crawled in there for shade. Suddenly I heard a ploop–ploop sound of something being dropped into the water. My eyes turned toward the nearby well in horror. Charlie KoKo was leaning over the side of the well dropping pebbles into it. I marched up to him trying to subdue the panic that was creeping like a snake in my veins.

'Charlie KoKo, have you seen Mi Koo? I can't find him anywhere.'

'Maaaaybe, maaaaybe not,' he replied with a wicked grin, teasing me as he usually did whenever he hid something precious of mine. Charlie was fond of playing practical jokes on Geok Poh and me. We both suffered extensively from his 'cruel' sense of humour and often got into trouble for missing school books, torn garments, broken combs, and disappearing cakes or biscuits.

'Charlie KoKo, you better tell me or I'll tell Tua Kor that you took her comb and use it on the dog,' I threatened.

'Go ahead, I still won't tell you what I've done with Mi Koo.'

'You better.' My voice was starting to rise. He continued to drop pebbles into the well and after an agonizing minute. 'Hei, look, what's this floating in the well.'

I rushed over and peered into the dark well.

'Oops, my mistake, that's a floating leaf, for a moment there I thought Mi Koo had resurfaced,' said Charlie. Had he thrown Mi Koo into the well!?

At that moment I lost it. I flew at Charlie, shook him fiercely and slapped him hard on the face. Charlie stumbled backwards, dragging me down with him. He struggled, but I pummeled him well.

'You wicked, wicked boy! *Eow siew, tay miah*,' I spit the death curse at him, my face turning purple as I glared at him still sitting on his stomach.

Cousin Charlie suddenly held up both his hands in surrender. 'Stop it, you vicious little tiger, I was just joking, jeez, Choo Choo Kor and my mom took him into the kitchen this morning.'

Breathlessly, I extricated myself from him and ran into the kitchen, where I heaved a sigh of relief. Charlie was telling the truth. Choo Choo Kor had had him the whole time. It looked like she was playing with him because she was holding a stick in front of him. Mi Koo strained his wrinkled neck out as he normally did when we played, and grasped the stick tenaciously. Choo Choo Kor pulled his head forward and Mi Koo held on, in what seemed like a tug of war between them. Tua Kor was standing impatiently next to Mi Koo watching Choo Choo Kor. I figured that she was probably waiting for her turn to play with the turtle because she kept hurrying Choo Choo Kor.

'Hurry up, Choo Choo-ah, I don't have all day,' Tua Kor said as she tapped her high heels impatiently on the wet cement floor.

'By the time you're done,' complained Tua Kor, 'Ah Choon's baby will be a year old.' Ah Choon was Tua Kor's precious daughter-in-law, her eldest son, Sunny Lim's wife. She had just given birth to a baby boy two weeks ago. I stood there puzzled, wondering what Ah Choon and her baby had to do with Mi Koo.

Both Choo Choo Kor and Tua Kor had their backs to me so neither of them knew that I was standing by the doorway watching.

There were no words to describe how I felt when I saw what Choo Choo Kor did next. I stood there like I was in a trance, a bystander watching a gruesome car wreck. I opened my mouth to scream, to stop her, but nothing came out. Everything happened in flashes. A sharp gleaming cleaver. The *WHACK* sound. Mi Koo's head, with his mouth still holding on tight to the stick, rolling towards the corner of the kitchen. Blood everywhere.

I turned to ice. I couldn't feel my legs, and would have fallen if I had not caught sight of a miracle. Mi Koo. Mi Koo was alive and he was crawling toward me. My heart, which was filled with horror moments ago filled with joy. But as he got closer, the horror returned, worse than before. Mi Koo was still headless—little did I know that turtles don't die right away. It was at that moment that both my aunts realized I had been standing there.

My high-pitched scream sliced through the early morning air, so shrill and urgent that both women froze.

'No-o-o-o-o-o-o,' I shrieked with all my might, 'No! No! No! No! No! No!' I suddenly found my legs and ran towards Choo Choo Kor.

'I hate you! I hate you! I hate you!' I started crying. By that time everyone in the entire household was in the kitchen looking alarmed, wondering if someone had accidentally chopped off an arm or finger.

My mother peeled me off Choo Choo Kor, took me firmly by the arm and calmly led me out of the kitchen. I was still crying. I cried so much that I developed a fever that night.

After I had left the kitchen Choo Choo Kor continued as if nothing out of the ordinary had happened. She picked up Mi Koo's lifeless body. He had given up trying to crawl away. She dipped him in boiling water and started scraping off his exterior layer of skin, including his shell. She then proceeded to remove his shell by cutting along the groove on each side between the front and back legs with a sharp knife. Apparently this was the narrowest part of the shell. The tail, neck, and all four legs are attached to the top of the shell. She then proceeded to remove the bulk of the meat from the shell.

'Remember to save the heart and the liver,' instructed Tua Kor. At this point she also instructed Choo Choo Kor to remove all the fat from the turtle's meat. Choo Choo Kor did this by rolling back the skin and with a paring knife and her index finger she scraped out all the fat.

When Mi Koo's meat was nicely cubed, Tua Kor took over the cooking process. She dropped the meat together with some shitake mushrooms, some herbal roots, and a dash of rice wine into a pot of boiling water. She simmered this soup for several hours, stirring it every half an hour to make sure that the meat was tender.

That night I glared at Ah Choon as she slurped greedily at the turtle soup. Turtle soup was considered a very nutritious delicacy that was especially good for women after giving birth. Damn her, damn her baby, damn Choo Choo Kor, damn Tua Kor, I cursed them all silently in my heart.

After this incident, I was sullen for weeks. However, being a simple-minded child, I eventually began to put the Mi Koo incident behind me. That was, until the dawn of the Hungry Ghost Festival. Upon seeing the opera stage being built, people buying joss sticks and hell money, I suddenly had a flashback of Mi Koo. I wondered if Mi Koo's ghost was going to come back, or whether he had gone to turtle heaven.

# 8

# Do Not Eat Your Ancestor's Food

On the first day of the seventh lunar month in the Chinese calendar, the gates of Hell are flung open to allow the ghosts and spirits of the netherworld into the world of the living for a month of food, wine, and entertainment. During this month, street banquets and Chinese street operas are held to entertain the spirits.

According to legends, the gates of Hell are opened at the break of dawn on this day to let anguished souls return to earth, where they can visit their descendants and enjoy the feasts prepared in their honour. Ghosts without families also return and wander aimlessly across the earth. To avoid being harassed by these outcasts, my mother and aunts would offer sacrifices like roasted pig or duck to these homeless ghosts as well as to our ancestors.

'Remember,' said my Ah Gaik Chee, sternly shaking her finger at us, 'don't any of you kids dare touch the food that we put out.'

It was hard to resist all the sweets and delicacies, but not wanting to anger any of our ancestors, my sister and I stayed away from the food. Besides, we were told that after the ghosts had 'eaten' the food, it would be devoid of any taste. My mischievous Cousin Charlie, however, just had to do what he was told not to.

'Pssst, hei,' I heard a soft, yet insistent whisper. 'Ah Lian.'

I ignored him, pretending not to hear. Besides, I was in the midst of playing 'cooking' with my other cousin, Geok Poh.

'Swee Lian, Geok Poh,' the voice came again, more urgently this time. We both looked behind us and gasped. There standing by the offering table was my Charlie KoKo holding a piece of glutinous rice cake triumphantly in his hand.

'Charlie KoKo, wha . . .' my cousin Geok Poh exclaimed loudly.

'Shhhhh, keep your voice down,' whispered Cousin Charlie, looking around nervously at the kitchen door. 'My mom will hear you.'

Geok Poh closed her mouth with a snap. But I wasn't going to let him get away with eating the cake that I had been eyeing the whole day.

If I couldn't have it then Charlie couldn't either.

'You'll get into trouble when Tua Kor finds a cake missing from the plate.'

'No I won't,' he replied confidently. 'I'll just blame it on Choo Choo Kor.'

I knew he would get away with it too, because whenever anything in the house broke down, everyone always pointed their finger at poor Choo Choo Kor. If the toilet handle broke, Choo

Choo Kor was blamed—she probably broke it with her buffalo strength. If the basin got clogged, Choo Choo Kor was at fault. Choo Choo Kor was undeniably clumsy, but she didn't deserve to be blamed for everything and anything. Unfortunately, that was the way this household worked. Furthermore, knowing Tua Kor, she would have rather believed that Choo Choo Kor stole the cake than her 'can-do-no-wrong' child.

Unfortunately for Charlie, as he said this, Tua Kor entered the room and caught him red-handed.

'What do you think you are doing?' Tua Kor bellowed. 'Put that cake back at once!'

'Sss...orry,' Charlie faltered, unable to return his mother's furious gaze.

'Sorry? Sorrry? What do you mean sorry? You'll be truly sorry when great great-grandpa Cheah pays you a visit tonight,' shouted my Tua Kor angrily as she pulled Charlie by the ear and made him kneel down in front of the offering table.

She then lit some joss sticks and placed them in his hands.

'You better apologize properly to your great great-grandparents and hope that they did not take offence of what you just did.'

Charlie did as he was told and apologized to his mother again. 'I'm really sorry, ma, I won't do it again.'

Tua Kor humphed irritably, 'Just see that you don't.'

After Tua Kor left the room, Charlie looked at us with his bright little wicked eyes, wiped away his crocodile tears and promptly popped the remaining cake into his mouth.

During this month, all children were advised to remain indoors to avoid a meeting with or collision of souls with the evil spirits that lurked outside. For us girls it was easier to stay indoors, as we could always play with our dolls or make up some indoor games. Being deathly afraid of being lured into the kingdom of the dead, we didn't dare play outside. However, for a kid like Charlie who was used to playing outside and running about the streets, it was agonizing to remain indoors. Cousin Charlie became especially restless when Tua Kor forbade him to go swimming with his friends.

'During this month, hungry ghosts, especially those that have drowned, are out looking for children to pull under so they can take their place in hell,' Tua Kor explained to a sulky-looking Charlie. He didn't dare reply to Tua Kor, so he just hung his head looking miserable.

One afternoon, after having been cooped up for two whole days, he stole out of the house, went across to an Indian neighbour's yard and started playing marbles with his best friend, Muthu. It wasn't until dinner time that Tua Kor discovered Charlie missing.

'Charlie, Charlie, where are you?' shouted my Tua Kor as she ran upstairs and downstairs like a mother hen looking for her lost chick.

Upon hearing his mother from across the street, Charlie quickly sneaked quietly back into the house via the servant's entrance. Nobody heard him coming back. No one guessed that Charlie had sneaked out and back again.

That night Charlie tossed and turned, then lay on his back in bed, thinking about his escapade this afternoon. What if what they said was true? Could he have bumped into an evil spirit on his way back and not know it? What if 'something' followed him home? The moon was up and through a ray that had pierced the darkness of the room, he thought he detected movement behind his bedroom door.

What was happening to him? Was he going mad? Was he being punished for being disobedient? Was a spirit trying to take over his body? He lay perfectly still with his eyes closed, hoping that the feeling would go away. But it didn't. It got worse.

At last it got so bad that he began to tremble and sweat. His body felt like it was on fire yet he shivered. Charlie got out of bed slowly and made his way to the door, as if walking in his sleep. He passed through the door like a ghost in pajamas.

How he found his way to Tua Kor's room he never remembered. Tua Kor awoke suddenly from her sleep to the soft yet insistent knocking on her bedroom door. She didn't answer immediately, what if it was a ghost. She wasn't about to extend an invitation for evil spirits to come in.

'Who is it?' she cried. But nobody replied. Tua Kor poked the sleeping figure next to her. Tua Tneow gave a loud grunt and flipped over, still snoring, unperturbed by his wife's jabbing. Tua Kor shook him more violently and this time he woke up.

'Huh? Whhaaaat?' he enquired sleepily.

'I heard a knock,' said Tua Kor in a hushed voice. 'When I asked who it was, nobody answered.'

'Maybe it was the wind,' Tua Tneow suggested, reluctant to get up from his comfortable bed. Then he heard it too, the soft tap, tap, tap on the door. That made him sit up straight. He looked around for the stick that he usually kept by his bed in case robbers came into the house.

He found it, got out of bed and went to the door, a short figure clad in a white T-shirt and a checkered sarong. He flung the door open and found a crumpled body at the foot of the door.

'Charlie! Charlie! What's the matter? Are you ill?' cried Tua Tneow as he threw down his stick and stooped down to help Charlie up, pulling him gently into the room.

'I, I, I don't feel well,' said Charlie, in a tired whisper. 'I'm scared.'

Tua Kor was very distraught. Charlie himself was frightened and confessed to his parents about his little afternoon escapade. The very next morning, Tua Kor took Charlie to a nearby temple to perform a simple religious ritual to rid him of the evil spirits that had touched him.

Upon arrival, Tua Kor proceeded to buy a bundle of joss sticks and a stack of square-shaped silver paper money made especially for the dead. Holding the lighted joss sticks in one hand and the paper money in the other, she started to burn the 'money' while waving it in circles before Charlie.

This act was also accompanied by uttering some prayers. Just before Tua Kor's fingers got burnt, she directed Charlie to spit on the burning paper money before discarding it to the ground. She then handed Charlie the set of joss sticks to stick in the ground and then instructed him to walk straight back home without casting a backward glance. Charlie did as he was told. Tua Kor then went the opposite direction, stopping at a coffee shop to meet a friend before going home. This ritual was done in hopes that the evil spirit would be so engrossed in counting the 'money' that he or she would lose track of Charlie and leave him in peace to recover.

The ritual worked because the very next day Charlie KoKo was back to his normal self again.

After having witnessed Charlie's affliction, my mother and Jee Kor decided that it was safer to protect Geok Poh and me before the same thing happened to us. We were taken to the same temple and each had a blessed yellow string fitted around her wrist.

On the fifteenth day of the Hungry Ghost month, we had to be especially careful. Many people stayed at home on this day to avoid an unlucky encounter with a ghost out enjoying the festival.

'Lian ah, please remember to look after your sister and not let her wander out to the riverbank, it's getting dark,' my mother would remind me. We had a river behind our house and therefore, had to take extra precautions to avoid walking near the riverbank where a water spirit could easily steal our body.

Despite all the precautions we had to observe during the *Phor Thor* Festival (Hungry Ghost Festival) the one thing I love about this month is the Chinese opera shows.

We kids also loved the vibrant carnival-like atmosphere that surrounds the stage where the opera was being set up.

Charlie's favourite game was *tikam*, which literally meant 'stab'. Whenever he saw this game, he had to try his luck.

'Oh please, please, please let me win the big prize,' prayed Charlie loudly one afternoon when we were at the carnival during the Hungry Ghost month. He clasped his hands together in a praying motion after he paid up and then selected a ticket from the board. He then slowly opened it up to see what prize he had won.

'Damn it, another bubble gum,' he complained.

'If you don't want it, give it to us.' I pointed to Geok Poh and myself. We both loved bubble gum, especially the one with the tattoo sticker.

Charlie tossed the gum to us and both Geok Poh and I split it with glee.

'Cheh cheh, I want ice cream.' Mei Mei pulled at my dress as she pointed to the ice cream stall. I had completely forgotten that Mei Mei was with us.

'Ok I will get you one if you promised to eat it slowly and not shove the whole thing into your mouth like you did last time and vomited it all out,' I warned her. Mei Mei nodded obediently as I ordered her a vanilla ice cream sandwiched between two wafer biscuits.

'Do you want to split one too?' I asked Geok Poh as she was busy blowing her bubble gum. She shook her head no, but she pointed to the Roti Bak Kwa stall where there was freshly grilled Chinese pork jerky nestled between soft warm steamed buns. She and I both loved this salty-sweet dried meat.

After filling our stomachs, we walked around to see what else was there, it was still early. Perhaps we could spin the wheel and win something.

Geok Poh suddenly had an idea. 'Come, let's try and peek behind the stage where the musicians and actors are.'

We walked toward the wings of the makeshift stage all excited. We could see a small band of musicians getting ready, testing their musical instruments.

'Come here, come here, lift me up a little,' instructed Geok Poh. I walked towards her and lifted her up.

'Tell me what do you see?' I asked excitedly.

'The actors and actresses are so beautiful, I am not sure how to describe. Their headdresses are so glittery and they have very heavy make-up on,' whispered Geok Poh.

'Come on, let's just go find our spot,' I said as I lowered her back onto the ground.

We walked around searching for a good spot to watch the opera. Each of us was holding our own little plastic stool. Suddenly we spotted Ah Hwa Chee, Ah Gaik Chee, and Choo Choo Kor, who had reserved a small area for us by placing a woven mat on the ground. We happily walked over to them. The show was about to start as the sun was setting.

The stage was brightly lit with fluorescent tubes and spotlights. I was mesmerized. I could not turn my eyes away from the elaborate costumes. The male actors had long beards and spoke in low growling voices, while the actresses would fling the silk extensions attached to their sleeves in feminine gestures, speaking in melodic tunes. The story usually revolved around war, murder, betrayal, and love. I could not understand a single word the performers were saying, but I just absolutely loved their expressions.

After a month of restrictions and living in constant fear, we were all glad when the earthly party for the ghosts came to an end on the final day of the seventh lunar month. At the appointed time of closing, a Taoist priest would chant liturgies while holding a 'seven-star sword' to let the ghosts know that it was time for them to return to the underworld. When the gates were shut, the priest cupped his ears to avoid being deafened by the wail of the spirits lamenting their return to Hades. After the gates of Hades were closed, my mother and aunts would make a ritual offering of food at the main entrance of our home, lighting incense and burning paper money for my ancestors to use in the spirit world.

If you think that only during the month of the Hungry Ghosts that we were supposed to be extra careful you would be mistaken. Every part of my growing up, all the way from birth to adulthood, revolves around some ghost or some spirit or other. Not all were malevolent, mind you, there were benign spirits too. However, lo and behold, if you accidentally offended them, they could turn nasty and curse you. There really was no place (or so it seemed) where you would not encounter a spirit or ghost.

Schools were no exception. Everyone knew that schools were hangouts of the infamous Hantu KumKum. This ghost especially loved to lurk in toilets, and that was why it was compulsory that we go to the toilet in pairs. I went to an all-girls school, and there were frequent reports of Hantu KumKum sightings by my classmates.

According to folklore, Hantu KumKum is a hideous old woman who roams around looking for young girls. She needs to drink their blood in order to restore her youth and beauty.

I was always afraid I would encounter her, so I would frequently insist that my 'toilet partners' stand right outside my door when I was using the toilet. The toilets at my school were in two long rows of cubicles, right across from each other, and you could enter from either end of the row. I usually stayed away from the middle cubicles because they were the furthest away from the sunlight and therefore the darkest. Also, if anything were to suddenly pop up, it would be quite a long run to escape to the end of the row.

By the way, the amulets that I was given for protection from evil spirits were rendered completely useless in toilets. We were advised never ever to wear them when going to toilets. That sucked big time because that was when we needed it the most!

According to my aunts, toilets were considered 'unclean' places. If I were to wear my amulet into them, the *angkong*, the deity which resides in the amulet, would run away. The explanation just didn't make any sense to me. Weren't these deities in the amulet supposed to protect me from ghosts?

Thankfully, throughout my school years I never encountered the dreaded Hantu KumKum. I did, however, experience the mystery of my screaming classmates.

It was a quiet Friday morning. Just like every other morning the *bus sekolah*, our school bus, always came really early.

'Swee Lian, Swee Lian, wake up!' Geok Poh shook me hard by the shoulders. 'The bus will be here in fifteen minutes, you have to hurry or we would miss it and get into deep trouble.'

I tried to open my eyes but felt really groggy. 'Few more minutes, let me sleep few minutes more,' I begged.

'No,' Geok Poh replied firmly, 'you know as well as I do that the Ah Pek bus driver is very impatient. We have to be ready the moment he arrives, otherwise we would get yelled at and he might even leave us behind.'

Our school bus always came early because he had to drop off so many kids in all the different schools. Unfortunately, we were the first ones he picked up at 5.00a.m. and as it happened, our school was the first one along his route, so we would also be dropped off the earliest. Being the first one to arrive in a dark empty school was no fun. Geok Poh and I were in the same grade but we were not in the same class, so we separated the moment we arrived at the premise.

On that Friday, as I hurried along the deserted corridors eager to reach my classroom, I felt the back of my neck prickle. Something was different, I didn't know what it was. When I arrived, the classroom was dark as expected, so I opened the door and went in, sliding my hand tentatively along the wall in search of the light switch.

To my surprise, when the light was turned on, I saw a figure sitting at the very back of the classroom. It was my friend, Munirah.

'Eh, Munirah, why are you here so early, for a moment there you gave me a scare.'

She turned to look at me but she had a puzzled look on her face, as if she could not comprehend what I was saying to her. It took her a moment before she replied in a flat voice, 'Hey, Swee Lian.'

I went closer to her and sat down in the chair in front of her. 'Are you okay, Munirah?'

She looked up again for a long while before replying, 'No, I think I am possessed by spirits.'

The hair on my arms stood up as I looked at her. I wanted so badly to just run for my dear life.

'These spirits have been following me for a while, I can't eat or sleep properly, also when I study, nothing goes in. I cannot remember anything at all. I am very worried because our final exams are coming up in a week,' she continued.

I did not know what to say, I was even afraid to hug her, fearing she might go all 'exorcist-like' on me. I just reached out and patted her hand, telling her not to worry and that it was just stress.

However, I will never forget what I saw later that day. Out of the blue, during our history class, Munirah fell to the ground and started screaming uncontrollably. No one knew what to do, we were all too afraid, we just stood there staring. Suddenly two more of my Malay classmates let out blood-curdling screams and fell to the ground, thrashing their bodies. It was one of the most frightening moments of my life.

What happened next was all a blur, students were pushing each other and rushing to the door trying to escape from the room. Teachers were trying to push in to see what was happening. Pandemonium broke out. As I was trying to get out, I could see from the corner of my eye the girls kicking and screaming as some of the teachers tried to approach them.

For months after that incident I had nightmares and dreaded going to school. I did, however, reached out to Munirah and visited her in her home, two weeks after the incident. She looked calm and even told me what happened to her that day.

'My parents dropped me off earlier than usual that Friday because they had to *balik kampung*, go back to their hometown Ipoh to visit my grandmother in the hospital. As I was walking towards our classroom, I caught a glimpse of a dark shadowy figure near the entrance of the toilet. I tried to look away but I couldn't and my feet felt heavy—almost like they were glued to the cement. I could not move as fast as I wanted to. The figure turned toward me and I could see it was an old lady, very, very old, her face was all wrinkled and she had a toothless smile. She motioned for me to come to her. I had seen her before, this is

not the first time. I started chanting a prayer in my heart, when I did so I think her spell broke for a moment.'

I scooted closer and put my arm around Munirah as she continued her story.

'I ran all the way to our classroom and just sat there. But I felt strange like I was in a dream. Suddenly I felt someone behind me and I turned my head to see who it was and everything went dark. Then I heard my name being called. That was you, you pulled me back by calling me. I thought everything was going to be okay, but later on that morning, I suddenly felt cold, really cold. I felt a fear too. There was a sharp pain in my chest, I could not breathe properly then it seemed like I was looking into another world. A world different from ours, I saw a face, the face of that old woman again. She looked evil. Pure evil. I tried to scream but no sound came out. Again I was paralyzed and that's when I passed out I think. I had no memory of what happened next.'

Munirah had tears rolling down her cheeks as she related her experience to me. I was crying too. I just held her tight, not really knowing how to comfort her.

After a while she told me not to worry as her parents had taken her to a *bomoh*, a spiritual healer, who abides by the teachings of the Quran, the Islamic holy book.

'He's been guiding me,' said Munirah with a smile, 'and I am feeling a lot better.'

That night as I was lying in bed, I thought to myself, in spite of the many possible 'disasters' that could have happened to me and the variety of 'strange' things that I have encountered while I was growing up, I think I did pretty well. I managed to survive my childhood—never been possessed by evil spirits (touch wood) nor was I ever caught by the infamous drain lady, or encountered a ghost during the seventh lunar month or became a snake during that one time I was too lazy to sit up while eating my biscuits. And thank goodness, the watermelon seed that I once swallowed by accident didn't grow into a plant inside.

# 9

# Paper Lanterns,
# Mooncakes, and a Wedding

After the Hungry Ghost month comes the Lantern or Moon Cake Festival, which is celebrated on the fifteenth day of the eighth month of the lunar calendar. Every year my mother and aunts would get together and make a special kind of moon-shaped sweet cake. These mooncakes were filled with red bean paste, lotus seeds, and duck eggs.

'Ma, why do we eat mooncakes during this month?' I remember asking my mother one day.

'I don't really know when the custom really began,' Ma replied. 'Perhaps you should ask one of your aunts.'

So I decided to ask my Tua Kor about it. I looked up to her, in my eyes she knew many facts about many things.

'I think it all started during the fourteenth century,' she replied thoughtfully. 'During that time China was fighting against the Mongols.'

'What happened then?' I asked curiously.

'Chu Yuen-Chang and his senior deputy, Liu Po-Wen, were discussing battle plans, and a secret strategy involving the mooncake was developed.' Tua Kor pondered for a while, trying to recall the story. 'I think it was said that Liu entered the city dressed up as a Taoist priest bringing along with him the moon cakes and distributed them to the residents there.'

Tua Kor took a bite of the mooncake, as if for effect, before she continued, 'So guess what the people found when they bit into their cakes?'

'A message?' I answered cautiously.

'Yes, they found the hidden messages and that's how the emperor won and took back the city,' replied Tua Kor. I am not sure if this version is true but regardless of whether the stories were true or not, as kids we still enjoyed sitting around the table eating moon cakes and pomelo fruit while Tua Kor told us moon-related stories. I remember another story was about the 'first lady on the moon'.

'Wasn't it an American astronaut named Neil Armstrong the first man to land on the moon?' protested one of my older cousins.

'Yeah, he landed on July 20th, 1969, I remember the teacher telling us about it at school,' yet another cousin chimed in.

The rest of us remained silent for we didn't know whom to believe. In the end, my oldest aunt, by virtue of her seniority, managed to convince some of us that her version was the truth.

This is how my Tua Kor's version of the somewhat complicated moon-landing story goes:

'A long time ago, in the Hsia dynasty there, lived a beautiful woman named Chang-O. Her husband was a skilled archer, named General Hou-Yi of the Imperial Guard. One day the emperor commanded General Hou to shoot down eight of the nine suns that had mysteriously appeared in the sky.'

'I don't think anyone can shoot the sun from the sky,' protested Charlie.

'Sshhh be quiet,' I turned and looked at Charlie, annoyed at the interruption.

Tua Kor continued as if she had not heard what Charlie had said.

'The General was richly rewarded and became very famous. However, the villagers were afraid that the suns might appear again. If it did it would make the earth very hot and possibly dry up all the water from the planet.'

'Never heard of nine suns before,' Charlie grumbled beneath his breath.

Tua Kor got irritated this time. 'Do you want to hear the story or not, if you don't then please just leave,' she scolded her son.

Charlie just kept quiet and looked sulkily at the floor.

Tua Kor continued, 'Because they were so afraid, they started praying to the Goddess of Heaven to make the General immortal. They wanted him to always defend them.'

'Did the Goddess grant their wish?' asked Cousin Geok Poh.

'Yes she did,' Tua Kor replied, 'their wish was granted and she gave General Hou the pill of immortality.'

At this point I can't remember exactly how Tua Kor told the story. But apparently, somehow the General's wife Chang-O (or was it Chang-e) got hold of the immortality pill and fled to the moon, taking her pet rabbit with her for company. When she landed on the moon, she coughed up the pill and instructed her apparently very smart rabbit to pound it into small pieces so that she could scatter them on earth and make everyone immortal (I have a feeling she didn't quite succeed). Anyway, as the story goes, she built a palace for herself and remained on the moon. For her attempt to make us immortal I guess my aunts and the rest of the Chinese population decided to honour them by stamping images of Chang-O and sometimes the Jade Hare on every moon cake.

My aunt's story didn't quite make sense but it did entertain us. Furthermore, if she kept telling us stories we wouldn't have to go to bed yet.

'Tua Kor, that was a good story, please tell us more,' my sister pleaded in her sweetest voice.

'It's almost time for bed,' my mother protested. 'You have school tomorrow, I don't want you to be tired. You get very grouchy and whiny when you don't get enough sleep.'

'Oh, it's all right, I'm sure just one more story won't hurt them,' said my Tua Kor, and as usual my mother, being younger and therefore lower in rank, relented.

The next story that Tua Kor told us was 'The Old Man on the Moon'. According to Chinese belief, marriages are made in heaven and prepared on the moon. This old man is supposed to be the one who does the preparing. It is also said that he keeps a record book with all the names of newborn babies. Therefore, he is the only heavenly person who knows everyone's future partners.

'So no one can challenge him?' I couldn't help but ask.

'Yup, no one could challenge him. Once it is written down in his book, no one can fight his decision,' replied Tua Kor patiently.

'So why do we have to carry lanterns?' asked Geok Poh.

'I guess, during this day when the moon is at its brightest, all children are encouraged to carry lanterns to celebrate him in hopes that he will see you and grant your wishes,' Tua Kor replied.

'Now for a treat before you go to bed,' Tua Kor said with a smile as she beckoned Choo Choo Kor to bring a tray filled with cups of warm freshly boiled barley water sweetened with rock sugar with bits of wintermelon in them and a handful of *too knia nah,* enough for all of us. Our eyes lit up as we stood up and hurriedly grabbed the brown cakes, which were shaped like piglets packed in little red baskets.

These cakes were not only delicious but also the right size for us to easily handle them without making a big mess. They fit into our small hands and mouths perfectly.

As usual, while stuffing his mouth with the entire piggy mooncake, Charlie asked, 'Why are these mooncakes shaped like piglets and why is there no filling in them?'

My heart leapt as I anticipated another story that would accompany this question. However, to my disappointment, Tua Kor just replied, 'Oh, those piglets are made from leftover dough from the mooncakes, we just didn't want to throw the unused dough away.'

'Why make it in the shape of a pig?' insisted Charlie, not letting her get away without an answer of that part of his question.

Tua Kor just shrugged and said, 'Don't know.'

After we washed down our brown cakes with barley water, Tua Kor shooed us off to bed.

I love mid-autumn festivals, as there were hardly any taboos that I had to be aware of. Kids were just free to enjoy themselves, carrying our painted cellophane lanterns and eating mooncakes.

Mid-autumn was also a time when many marriages took place since it was right after the 'ghost' month, and everyone knew there were no weddings held during that month.

The next exciting thing that happened after the mooncake festival was a wedding. It was my first wedding ever, and it was happening right next door. My neighbour's daughter, whom I addressed as Vivian Chee because she was older than me, was getting married. My neighbours, Mr and Mrs Teoh, were also Peranakans, but somehow they were a little different from my family. Not so much in terms of the customs that they observed but rather in the way they spoke—they used a lot more Malay words then we did. I think I heard someone mention that they were originally from another state called Malacca.

They had asked my grandparents if they could also use our house during the festivities especially for the *chnia lang kek,* which is the banquet for the guests. I figured they must have invited more guests then their own house could accommodate. Of course, Ah Mah and Ah Kong gladly agreed.

One Thursday evening, two days before the wedding, Geok Poh and I were playing *chit liap buah* (seven stones), a game of 'grab the stones'. It was a simple game that required skill, agility, and seven small stones. First you hold all seven stones in one hand, second you toss all of them onto the ground, then you pick up one, throw it into the air and at the same time pick up as many stones on the ground before catching the one that was thrown. Geok Poh and I practised this game diligently until we were able to throw one stone in the air and successfully pick up all six in one sweep.

Anyway, we were playing on the patio when suddenly Ah Gaik Chee appeared all excited, breathing very fast and red in the face.

'Ah Lian, Geok Poh, hurry, hurry, the *berandam* is about to begin. Come, come, let's go over and watch.'

'What's *berandam*?' I asked, puzzled.

'It's the ritual of combing and trimming the bride's hair,' Ah Gaik Chee replied.

I got up, eager to go, but Geok Poh said she wasn't interested, so she stayed behind.

Ah Gaik Chee and I peeped into the bedroom of the bride where the *berandam* ritual was taking place. We could see her Auntie Mary and the hairdresser (who was also the mistress of ceremonies) combing Vivian Chee's fringe and tying it into two tiny tufts with white ribbons on both sides of her forehead.

Ah Gaik Chee whispered softly to me, 'White ribbon means the bride is pure, still a virgin lah.' I nodded although I did not truly comprehend what 'virgin' means. Then she continued in her 'know it all' voice albeit still whispering, 'look look you see if the hairline along the forehead is curl-curl, comb also cannot do anything, it means the girl no longer pure, means got "experience".'

Vivian Chee looked really beautiful to me. In my heart I wished to be like her when I grew up, and at that moment I also decided that I would sport a fringe.

The next day, Friday, was the wedding eve. I could see and hear the servants next door, all in a frenzy, cleaning the big hall next door which was to be used only for the wedding. Since Ah Kong and Ah Mah had promised to let them use our hall, our home was also in a similar state of cleaning frenzy since early that morning. Today was the day when the *chnia lang keh*, banquet for the guests, was to be held.

A long rectangular table called the *t'ng tok* (Long table) was set up for the feast. Cooks were hired by the Teohs specially to prepare today's food. For almost a week prior to today, preparations had been underway. I remember the sound of pounding and the smells of shallot and different spices being made from scratch.

At around 10 a.m., cars were starting to roll up in the Teohs' driveway, dropping off ladies all decked out in beautiful kebayas and cheongsams.

Fascinated by all the goings-on, I hung around the Teohs' house watching Mrs Teoh instruct her servants to serve the ladies longan tea as they were ushered into a room where a game or cherki, a card game, was already in session. Before lunch I saw the servants bringing them bowls of chicken macaroni soup. I licked my lips, wishing I too could have a bowl. Chicken macaroni soup was one of my favourite soups other than lotus root soup.

Feeling bored, I decided to go home and inspect the food that was laid out on the *t'ng tok*. I hoped there would be leftovers for us too. I saw Tua Kor hovering over the table making sure that everything was perfect for the ladies' luncheon. Apparently only the ladies were invited for lunch, and only the men were invited for dinner. I couldn't help myself any longer—the fragrant smells wafting from the table were taunting me. I wandered over to the table and looked at each dish.

The first dish that caught my eye was kari kapitan, a chicken curry dish that has a slightly tangy sour taste of kaffir lime leaves. Rich with coconut milk and laden with a plethora of herbs and spices, the taste of this robust gravy is unmistakable. The second dish that caught my eye was the lobak (three-layer pork that has been marinated with five spice powders and wrapped in bean curd sheets).

'Hey what are you doing?' Charlie KoKo asked as he came up behind me suddenly.

'Nothing, just looking at all the delicious food,' I sighed wishing I could sample some of them. To my horror, he suddenly picked up one of the pieces of lobak and popped it into his mouth.

'Your mom would freak out if she saw you,' I exclaimed in disbelief at what he just did.

Charlie just kept on chewing his lobak and smiled, walking further down the table to inspect the other dishes. The next few dishes were the *assam koh hae* (tamarind paste fried prawns) and the *gulai tumis*, a type of curry fish that has a thick sourish gravy. There was nothing that I particularly liked, and the last dish that I liked even less than all the other dishes was the Nyonya *chap chai*, a stir-fried mix vegetables dish that has gingko, broccoli, mushrooms, carrots, and cauliflower. Charlie stuck his finger into one of the curry fish dishes, winked at me, licked his finger, and hurried off before anyone could catch him. I did not bother telling on him, since he often got away with it anyway.

As I was about to walk away, Choo Choo Kor motioned me towards the kitchen. As I entered the kitchen, my eyes opened wide with glee as my gaze fell upon the marble kitchen table laden with Nyonya desserts, or *chochi mulut,* as my Ah Mah called them. According to my grandma, as Peranakans, we must always finish a meal with a sweet dessert.

Choo Choo Kor held out a place of kuih to me.

'Nah, this I specially saved up for you. It is those that are not presentable enough to be served to guests.'

I looked down and saw that the desserts that were on the plate were odds and ends of each kind of kuih.

I smiled up at Choo Choo Kor. 'Thank you, thank you, thanks so much for saving these for me.'

'Don't let any of your aunts or grandma see you or I will get into trouble.'

'I will be careful,' I promised her.

'Take this,' she instructed as she took a piece of napkin and handed it to me. 'Cover it up.'

Carefully holding the plate with both hands, I slowly made my way upstairs. I was heading for my bedroom when Geok Poh suddenly appeared.

'Hey Swee Lian, you are back already? I thought you were still at Uncle and Auntie Teoh's place,' Geok Poh asked as she looked at my napkin-covered plate with curiosity. 'What do you have there?'

'Sssshhh, not so loud.' I placed a finger on my lips, then pointed toward my bedroom door, gesturing for her to follow me into the bedroom.

Just as we were about to sit down and unveil the plate there was a knock on the door. We both nearly jumped out of our skins and I almost dropped the plate. Thank goodness I did not. The knock came again, this time more urgently followed by Jee Kor's voice asking, 'Eh why lock door, who's in there? Lian are you in there? Is Geok Poh with you? I have been looking all over for her.'

I knew we had to answer or we would be in big trouble. I unlocked the bedroom door to let Jee Kor in. 'Yes, Geok Poh is here with me.'

As Jee Kor entered, her sharp eyes immediately spotted the plate. She walked over and picked up the napkin from the plate.

To my surprise, instead of scolding us, she sat down, smiled and said with a twinkle in her eye. 'Come, share your kuih with me and I won't tell Tua Kor.'

There was plenty, we were more than happy to share.

Jee Kor picked up a piece of *apom bokwa* and stuffed it into her mouth. This fluffy soft-yeasted pancake was made from fermented rice flour, its middle tinged with juice from blue pea flowers. The sauce in which we dip it, is made from fresh coconut milk, palm sugar, and topped with golden yellow *pengat pisang* (bananas). As she munched on her dessert, Jee Kor pointed to the bananas and explained, 'This golden yellow bananas are deemed to be auspicious, that's why this pancake is made specially for weddings.'

Geok Poh and I decided to share one *kau chan kuih* (nine-layer dessert) where each layer can be peeled and eaten. The layers in this chewy pudding-like cake is made of a set of three colours, orangey-red, pink, and white. The layers alternate between these colours.

'Does each of these kuihs have a special meaning?' I asked Jee Kor as I continued to shove the cakes into my mouth.

'Yes,' Jee Kor nodded. 'But basically all of them carry an auspicious meaning so the happy couple can lead a happy, healthy, and prosperous life.'

The three of us enjoyed our secret cake-eating session and for the rest of the day we were in a good mood. Nearing the evening I could see cars rolling up onto the Teohs' driveway again. This time, men all dressed up in suits, coats and ties arrived.

Unliked the ladies who arrived for lunch and were ushered in immediately, the men lingered outside the house while waiting for dinner.

'Why don't they go in?' I asked Ah Gaik Chee who was beside me, also peeking through the glass window panes.

'The guests usually take their seats when the serunee band plays for the third time,' she explained. 'Do you know that each dish has a tune of its own?'

'Really?' I said in disbelief.

'Yes different tunes are played depending on which dish is being served,' Ah Gaik Chee said, amused by my puzzled look.

I got bored waiting and went off to find my little sister to play *masak-masak* (a cooking game) with.

I couldn't find Mei Mei anywhere, so I came back and sat down beside Ah Gaik Chee again.

'Listen, listen!' She looked at me with excitement gleaming in her eyes.

I strained my ears to hear and I could hear the drums becoming louder and the tempo of the band quickening.

'You hear that?' asked Ah Gaik Chee. 'That's the signal for the guests to leave the table.'

As the guests were walking out to the compound, I saw the bride for the first time, all dressed up. Beside her was the *sang kheh umm,* the same older lady who had dressed her and helped her comb her hair.

'She is the one that teaches Vivian Chee how to kneel, walk, and seat properly and gracefully,' Ah Gaik Chee explained to me as she pointed at the woman.

I looked at Vivian Chee and thought it was so weird the way she folded her arms and kept her eyes downcast. It seemed so unnatural. Even the way she walked was weird, swaying in from left to right.

'Why does she walk like that?' I turned to ask Ah Gaik Chee.

'Oh, well it is believed that this movement would ward off any clashes with the evil spirits.'

'Tonight there is another ceremony, an initiation ceremony,' Ah Gaik Chee informed me. 'Do you want to watch?'

My eyes gleamed with excitement. 'Can Cousin Geok Poh and Mei Mei come too?'

After some pondering, Ah Gaik Chee agreed to let Geok Poh come but not Mei Mei. 'Mei Mei is too young, besides, she might snitch on us. You know how she is, always telling tales and "reporting" to your mom.'

That day after midnight we snuck out. The three of us went in through the backdoor—the servants at Mr and Mrs Teoh's house were good friends with Ah Gaik Chee, so they left the back door unlocked for us.

We arrived just in time to see Vivian Chee stepping onto a large bamboo tray. 'What's she doing?' I whispered, puzzled. 'Why is she getting into that big tray and sitting on that wooden thing that we use to measure rice?'

'The thing that she is seating on is called the *gantang*,' Ah Gaik Chee explained. 'Only virgins can sit on it and the round tray symbolizes the world.'

'But why?' I asked again impatiently.

'Shhhh, just watch, I'll explain later,' said Ah Gaik Chee, but I persisted.

'What are those items for?' This time it was Geok Poh who asked, pointing at the objects on the floor: a weighing scale, a pair of scissors, a mirror, a red thread and a razor.

'Sssshhhh.' Ah Gaik Chee put her finger to her lips. 'I told you I will explain later, you don't want us to be caught, do you?'

Geok Poh and I shook our heads and just watched as the objects were handed one by one to the boy standing there and then the boy would hand them over to Vivian Chee.

We both watched with fascination even though we did not fully comprehend what was going on.

Later as we were walking back to the house, Ah Gaik Chee explained, 'The scales are to remind Vivian Chee to weigh her actions and act justly. The scissors I think is for her to make things equal between her husband and herself, the razor is to remind her to be cautious in all that she does, and the mirror is there so that she can discern good deeds from bad deeds.'

'What about the comb and the red thread?' I asked fascinated.

To my disappointment, Ah Gaik Chee did not know.

'Never mind, I will ask Tua Kor or Ah Mah tomorrow,' I said.

'No, no, you cannot ask them, if you do they will know that we have snuck out. If they find out I will never ever take you out anymore,' she threatened, fearing that if our midnight 'adventure' was discovered she would get into trouble and quite possibly a beating too.

'Both of you have to promise not to say anything.'

We both nodded.

I went to bed that night filled with wonderment, thinking to myself, wow, we Peranakans sure are complicated people. How am I supposed to learn all the traditions and rules and taboos?

The next morning I was awakened by the loud sounds of firecrackers being set off.

'*Knia sai kau liao, knia sai kau liao*,' chanted Mei Mei as she jumped on my bed and shook me violently, announcing that the groom had arrived.

I hopped out of bed excitedly. Still in my home-sewn pajamas, I ran to the balcony that overlooked the front porch of the Teohs' mansion. I saw the groom walking up to the main door and there was a pageboy waiting there to present him with an orange on a silver saucer. The groom then waited there patiently until he was invited in by an elder, who performed the ceremonial greeting of *knia lay* so that he could enter the Teoh household.

As the groom disappeared into the house, I quickly rushed to change out of my pajamas. Mei Mei, all dressed up, was very excited and kept asking me to hurry up. While I was brushing my teeth, Geok Poh entered.

'You better hurry up, Tua Kor has given us permission to go over next door to watch.'

'Okay, okay,' I replied, my mouth still foaming with toothpaste.

As both of them were staring at me impatiently, I decided to forgo brushing my hair.

The three of us ran downstairs, put on our shoes and went over next door. Using the servants' entrance in the kitchen we went upstairs towards the bridal chamber. As we were making our way up the stairs, we could see the groom being served tea as he waited for the *chim pang* ceremony to begin. I remembered Ah Gaik Chee had told me that in this ceremony the couple would meet for the first time.

I lingered for a moment at the staircase, briefly wondering what the groom might be thinking, meeting his bride for the first time. Was it an exciting moment? I wondered. My head was filled with romantic thoughts about their eyes meeting for the first time and it was love at first sight and all that Mills and Boon romance novel stuff that I had read.

However, as I took a second glance at the groom, I couldn't help but wince, for he was nothing like I imagined as described by all those romance books. He was not tall, dark, and handsome with 'sinewy' muscles. I was disappointed and felt a little sorry for Vivian Chee. Her husband-to-be looked rather stocky, sporting a bald spot at the top of his head, and he wore horn-rimmed glasses. His complexion was pasty, quite pale in fact, like someone who had never been in the sun before. Suddenly, my thoughts were interrupted when I felt Mei Mei tugging at my blouse.

'Cheh cheh, faster come see the bride.'

I hurried after her, just in time to see the bride's parents covering her head with a black net-veil. Vivian Chee looked very solemn and she hardly smiled even when she saw us peeking at her from outside her bedroom door. Her eyes seemed to be red and brimming with tears. I felt a little sad as I looked at her. I guess I would be sad too if I had to leave my parents behind and go live with someone else. Being married also meant we were no longer children. Perhaps this 'happiest day' of a girl's life isn't all that it's cracked up to be.

Suddenly Choo Choo Kor appeared and ushered us away from the door, saying that my mother was looking for me and my sister. I turned to Ah Gaik Chee and made her promise that she would tell me the details of what happened after we left.

That night before bedtime I pestered Ah Gaik Chee to fulfill her promise.

'Well, after you left the groom came up and invited the bride to come out. They were both then served with tea and a bowl of red and white *kueh ee* (glutinous rice balls),' she said.

'What's the significance?' I asked.

'Apparently this signifies that the newly-wed couple will be blessed with sweetness in their life,' Ah Gaik Chee explained after some thought. 'Oh and another strange thing was that the remaining *kueh ee* were placed under the bridal bed, apparently it will remain there until the twelfth day of the wedding.'

At some point I must have lost interest because the next day I did not rush over to the Teohs' house to look or participate in the festivities. I didn't think anything much was happening anyway because on the third day I saw Vivian Chee and some of her older Nyonya aunties leaving in their cars (which were loaded with gifts of food) to visit her in-laws.

The festivities went on for the next few days, but since Geok Poh, Mei Mei, and I were too young to be involved, we just kept to ourselves. On the twelfth day, which was the last day of the wedding celebration, we were in for a surprise. Tua Kor woke us up early that day.

'Wake up, wake up, faster, get dressed in your finest clothes. I am going to take you out. We have been invited to join the festivities in the groom's house.'

Still in a daze but feeling excited at the same time we got out of our beds, brushed our teeth, combed our hair, and changed into dresses that had been laid out for us.

'This dress is so itchy,' I complained to Geok Poh. I hated wearing dresses; somehow I felt exposed when I wore skirts or dresses.

Anyway we hurriedly ate our breakfast, taking huge bites of our buttered toast dipped in half-boiled eggs and soy sauce and then gulping down our cups of hot Milo.

Piling into Tua Kor's car, we made our way to the groom's house. Upon arrival we were instructed by Tua Kor to hold onto each other tightly so as not to get lost in the crowd, and to follow her closely. I reached out my hand and held onto Mei Mei; Mei Mei in turn held on to Geok Poh's left hand, and Geok Poh used her right hand to hold on to Tua Kor's handbag. We followed Tua Kor single file like baby ducklings behind their mother.

We came to a room with a huge bed in it. I think that must have been the bridal bed, because it was all decorated. To our delight, as we entered we saw that there was a hen and a rooster in the room. The rooster and the hen were then released under the bridal bed. We were then each given a handful of rice grains and instructed to scatter them on the floor.

It was so much fun. As usual, I was impatient and threw all of mine in one throw, the way one might throw confetti, and immediately regretted it because then I had nothing left to do but stand there. Mei Mei and Geok Poh, on the other hand, were more cautious in throwing theirs. They scattered a little bit at a time as they walked in circles.

Since I had no more rice to throw, I squatted down and peered under the bed, looking at the rooster and the hen. To my surprise, I saw that there were other things under the bed like yam plants, bananas, and lemongrass.

I tapped on Tua Kor's arm to get her attention.

'Why are there those things under the bed?' I asked her I pointing under the bed.

'Oh those items are merely to symbolize fertility. Everyone, especially the bride and groom's parents are hoping that they would have a baby as soon as possible,' Tua Kor patiently explained to me.

It wasn't very long before the rooster came running out and started pecking on the rice grains. Everyone clapped, as this meant that the couple's first child would be a son. If the hen had emerged first, their child would have been a daughter.

After all the rituals, we were free to roam the house and mingle with the other children. The three of us wandered around till we came to the courtyard where there were groups of children playing a variety of games. Some were playing 'pick up sticks', while others were playing card games like Old Maid, Happy Family or Donkey. The older kids were running around playing 'catching,' a game where you have to freeze when the catcher taps you. Only when someone else who is not the catcher rescues (taps) you again, you can move. The downside of the game is that, sometimes you can be 'frozen' for a long time waiting for someone to come 'rescue' you.

Feeling a little shy, Mei Mei, Geok Poh, and I decided that we would just watch. At around 6 p.m., all the children were called indoors for dinner. Tonight was the *chia ching kay/chia che umm* dinner party, the night of culmination of the entire wedding ceremony. This dinner party was specially thrown by Vivian Chee's parents-in-law for her parents. Close family and all those that had assisted during the past twelve days were also invited to join the festivities. I guessed the reason why Ah Mah, Ah Kong, and the rest of us were invited—we had let them use our hall for the banquet. Anyway, whatever the reason, I was just happy we were invited to partake in the festivities.

# 10

# Spirit of the Coin and Hairdressers

My middle and late childhood years were my most interesting years, because that's when I held the 'power' to predict the future, or so I thought.

One day my sister, cousins, some neighbourhood kids, and I were playing 'spirit of the coin,' a cheap version of the Ouija board.

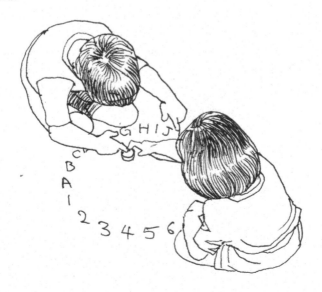

Almost every day after school, we would gather and ask the spirit *important* questions about our lives. Some of my questions were: What will I be when I grow up? The spirit 'spelled' out— T.E.A.C.H.E.R. (He/she/it was actually right on this one.) What are my husband's initials? The spirit spelled out B.K.N. After we were done asking questions, we would offer sugar to the spirit to go home.

Anyway, after this particular session, for the longest time, I searched for a boy with those initials. I looked for him everywhere. Being in an all-girls school made my search harder, if not near impossible, so I resorted to the next best thing. I started joining various clubs. First the swim team, then the Red Crescent Society, then table tennis club, and finally during my final year of high school, I joined the girl guides in hopes of meeting a boy scout with those initials. In spite of my best efforts, I wasn't successful.

When everything seemed hopeless, a friend of mine told me that if I lit a candle at midnight in front of a mirror I would be able to see the face of my future husband. That's easy enough, I thought to myself. Unfortunately, my parents weren't thrilled to find their little girl wandering in the middle of the night carrying matches and candles. So I never got to see B.K.N's face.

I soon got tired of trying to find him and settled for the knowledge of how old I would be when I married him and how many children we'd have. That information was easy enough to obtain, and I found it satisfying.

In order to find out how old I'd be when I finally married him, I had to pull out a strand of hair and tie it to a ring. I then held the ring next to a cup. Miraculously, the ring started moving, and soon it started to hit the rim of the cup. That part was crucial, because I had to count the number of hits. I was

up to '26' when the ring slowed down. Feeling fairly happy, for that wasn't too bad an age to be getting married, I proceeded to ask my friend to predict how many kids we'd have. She did it the only way we knew how—she took hold of one of my hands, gave it a hard slap and told me to close it immediately while she pressed hard on the base of my palm till some knobs appeared. She then counted them and said confidently, 'Well, you're going to have three kids.' And that was that.

My obsession with trying to find out about my future husband was probably influenced by my older cousins who were of marriageable age, and hence it was natural that they would be preoccupied with finding husbands. In retrospect, I wonder why, why were we girls so obsessed with getting married, acting like it was our life's goal. Looking at my grandparents' marriage, my own parents' marriage, and those of my relatives I was convinced that it was not at all a bed of roses.

One frequent source of quarrel was the love for gambling (for both men and women, we Peranakans do love to gamble). For the men in my family, it would be visiting the Penang Turf Club and betting on racehorses. For the women it would be *cherki* or mahjong. Once Ah Kong tried to control Ah Mah's gambling habits by cutting her weekly pocket allowance. This did not sit well with Ah Mah at all, and a huge fight ensued between them when it was discovered that she had resorted to pawning some of her jewellery to pay off her debts.

Another source of quarrel was the husbands' love of visiting the 'Worlds.' This was a sort of entertainment or amusement park. The one that my grandpa and uncles visited was called the New World. In the New World you could find anything and everything, and there were spectacular colourful sideshows all the time (or so I was told). They had ferris wheels, cabarets, open-air stages for singing, daredevil motorcycle stunts, Chinese operas, shooting galleries with air rifles, magicians, gaming stalls, hawker food stalls, and a variety of sundry shop stalls that sold a variety of merchandise. Apparently there was also a Peranakan *wayang* (opera) that performed the famous story of *Oh Chua Peck Chua* (Black Snake White Snake).

Looking at the list of entertainments above, I think the only thing the women were not too happy about was their husbands frequenting the cabarets. Who could blame them? No woman likes her man dancing with other women. One night after Ah Kong and two of his friends left for the World, I overheard Ah

Gaik Chee telling Choo Choo Kor and Ah Hwa Chee how unhappy Ah Mah was. They were gathered in the kitchen, and Ah Hoon Cheh was there too. I happened to come downstairs to get a hot drink before I went to sleep.

'I heard them having a bad fight before he left,' said Ah Gaik Chee.

'Yea, when I was helping her with her night clothes she was still crying,' added Ah Hoon Cheh.

'Do you know what happens in the cabarets?' asked Ah Hwa Chee innocently, being the youngest in that group.

'Usually men would buy dance coupons before they get to dance with the girls. I heard it is not cheap, $1 for three dances with one of the dance hostesses,' said Ah Gaik Chee. 'I also heard that some men have their 'favourites' and they would rush to those girls before each dance.'

'So Cheah Ko and his friends do that?' asked Choo Choo Kor.

'No, of course not, they are rich, they can book the cabaret girl by the hour. Once you book the girl, she will spend her time with just you lah.' Then she lowered her voice, looked around the room to make sure it was safe before continuing. 'I heard that he recently became infatuated with one of the girls there named Shirley, that's why he's been going every week,' said Ah Gaik Chee smugly.

'Who told you?' asked Choo Choo Kor skeptically. She had always had a soft spot for Ah Kong because he was kind to her.

'The *majie* next door lo, who else,' replied Ah Gaik Chee in exasperation, referring to our neighbors the Teohs' domestic helper.

'Apparently, he had been buying her things, they were seen shopping in Penang Road. Also seen in one of the hawker stalls near Gurney Drive having supper after midnight.' Ah Gaik Chee seemed to enjoy that she was privy to that information about Ah Kong.

'Remember that girl Ruby? The one whose lipstick is always super red and wears expensive cheongsams? Remember her? We met her during one of our visits to the Snake Temple, she told me she used to be a cabaret girl. I heard that she is now Tony Goh's father's mistress,' said Choo Choo Kor.

'Not uncommon, many rich businessman have mistresses, it is a symbol of their high status,' replied Ah Gaik Chee in a matter-of-fact way.

As I listened to their conversation I felt very uncomfortable. My Ah Kong was a very handsome man who often sported a sports jacket and hat, especially when he went out (though when he was at home, he wore a sarong). If memory serves, he mostly dressed in a very Western manner wearing cotton shirts and tie or bow tie when he goes to work or attend formal functions. This made him very attractive to women. I hoped he had not taken any mistresses. That would make Ah Mah very sad.

Other than my obsession with marriage, another obsession that I had during those years was my desire to change my name. Remember earlier on I mentioned that I really disliked my name? Now that I was older, I felt that I could actually make this happen. I remember trying desperately to change my name to Jill after watching episodes of Charlie's Angels. Farrah Fawcett was so beautiful. But no one would call me that, they even laughed at me. My grandma got upset at me for trying to change my name because she was the one who had chosen my name for me.

I could not understand why I was not given an English name. My Tua Kor had one—she was called Irene, after one of my grandpa's favourite songs, 'Goodnight Irene.' My Jee Kor had one too—she was called Nellie. Even my grandma had an English name. She was Rose, named after the song 'Rose, Rose, I Love You.' I felt left out.

My naive eleven-year-old brain figured that if I were to change my name to Jill and had a haircut just like Farrah, I would look just as beautiful. Ma must have felt sorry for me because when I asked her to take me for a haircut, she did so without questioning about it.

The haircut place was actually a house turned into something like a salon. I remember sitting there and looking directly into the kitchen at a stocky man wearing shorts and a Pagoda-brand singlet, cooking something that smelt like dead fish, rotten eggs, and sweaty armpits all rolled into one.

I felt sick but couldn't leave because this lady was going to make me look beautiful, just like Farrah Fawcett. So I made myself sit down and explained and explained and explained to her how I wanted my hair to be cut. I was positive she understood me, for the entire time that I was explaining, she was nodding and smiling. Then she took out a pair of sharp shiny scissors and began to cut.

When she was done, she whipped out a hand mirror and gave it to me. I looked into the mirror and the image of a Romulan with bangs cut short and straight across my forehead looked back at me. I didn't quite understand what went wrong that day until years later, when my mom told me that the lady only knew how to cut one style and one style only—that's why she charged so cheap.

When we got home, the only person that complimented me on my new hairstyle was Choo Choo Kor.

'Nice, nice, can see nice big ear now, hear better,' said Choo Choo Kor.

I scowled at her and lashed out rudely, 'What do you know? You are so ugly, so old, till now no husband, no boyfriend, no one want you?' Seriously, what did this drabby old lady who wears pink plastic barrettes, whose wardrobe consists of faded polyester tops and flowery pants, know about fashion anyway? As if that wasn't enough, I continued on spitefully, 'Lucky you have no kids too, you would make a bad mother.' I knew this would hurt her.

Recalling that incident I am now truly ashamed. If I had known then what I know now about my Choo Choo Kor's life, her 'secret', why she had no husband or children of her own, I would have treated her better and with more respect. But being a spoilt brat then I didn't know any better.

My Choo Choo Kor's life before she came to live with the Cheah family was very 'hush hush' (I think the older members of the family knew but not the younger ones). However, there were so many eyes and ears living under the same roof in our household that sooner or later, everything came out. Hardly anything could be kept a secret for very long.

Anyway, this was how I came to find out the true story about Choo Choo Kor.

Sometimes when my older cousins thought the younger ones were fast asleep, they would start talking about things that were supposed to be kept away from children's ears, our ears. As best I could, I would sometimes force myself to stay awake so I can hear all the 'juicy' details of their lives.

One day just after midnight, when my eyes were heavy with sleep and I was almost drifting off, I heard whispering. I slowly forced my eyes to open again but did not turn around. For a brief moment I entertained the thought that maybe it was some supernatural being whispering behind my back.

After listening for a few seconds I recognized my Ah Gaik Chee and Ah Hwa Chee's voices.

'Why are you crying?' Ah Gaik Chee said in a soft voice.

'Did you have a nightmare?'

'Was someone mean to you?' Ah Hwa Chee asked in a caring voice while patting Choo Choo Kor on her shoulders.

'How can someone be mean to her, she was crying in her sleep. Sometimes you ah, I really think you have no brains.' Ah Gaik Chee sounded very irritated as she scolded Ah Hwa Chee.

At that point I slowly turned over to face them. I closed my eyes again to the point where I could still peek out through the slits, but unless they took a closer look, they would still think that I was fast asleep.

I could see Choo Choo Kor's body hunched over, her hands cradling her head. Tears were streaming down her cheeks. She nodded. 'Yes, I dreamt of what happened before I was sent here.'

'Can you share with us?' Ah Gaik Chee prodded.

Choo Choo Kor paused for a moment and wiped her tears with the back of her hand before answering, 'I was about thirteen years old at that time when they took me. I didn't even have my period yet.'

Staring straight, as if in a trance, she continued, 'It happened one afternoon. I was on my way to do my tiffin food delivery to my mother's clients.' Her voice trailed off. 'It was my fault really, I took another route instead of the normal one. I wanted to stop by the corner *chai tiam mah* (sundry shop) to buy a packet of Marie Biscuits. I was stopped by two Japanese police officers.

'They asked me what was in the tiffin carrier, I told them my mom's homemade food. One of them asked me to open the cover, I obeyed and showed them the food in each tier. There were three tiers altogether. I still remember so clearly, as if it was just yesterday, the first tier consisted of stir-fried Chinese long beans with minced pork, the second layer had tau yew bak (braised pork belly in soy sauce), and the third one had lotus root soup with peanuts. The two officers licked their lips hungrily as they smelled the food. They then requested that I follow them to meet their Commander because he might want to order my mom's tiffin delivery service.

'I asked them if I could finish my deliveries first. They said no, I have to follow them now. When one of the officers saw that I was reluctant, he asked me if I was not interested in bringing more business to my mom. He said if the Commander decided to order tiffin food for all the soldiers and officers, my mom would get a lot of money.'

'I hope you didn't follow them,' Ah Gaik Chee said, looking earnestly at Choo Choo Kor. Even as she said it, she knew that it was impossible to say no to the Japanese officers. If Choo Choo

Kor had put up a fight she might have been killed or worse, her whole family would have been killed too.

Choo Choo Kor averted her eyes as she answered, 'I didn't really have a choice, although I did think that the officer made sense; if the Commander decided to cater from my mom, we would be rich.'

I held my breath as I continued to eavesdrop on Choo Choo Kor's story. She continued after wiping her tears on her pajama sleeve.

'The officers told me that their commander was stationed at a hotel located at the junction of Jalan Burma and Jalan Zainal Abidin. When we arrived they instructed me to put down my tiffin carriers and enter a room.

'I did as I was told, it took a moment for me to adjust my eyes as I entered, the room was dark, I thought it was weird to have an office in such a dark room. Before I could do anything else, I heard the door slammed shut and locked.

'At first I banged on the door screaming to be let out, I screamed till I had no voice left.

'I'm scared... I was so scared. I kept thinking of my mom and how worried she would be, not knowing what had happened to me.

'After what seemed like hours, the door opened and a Japanese official came in, I guessed he must be the commander. He was a short heavy-set man, with a moustache, and really bad breath.

'He said if I was obedient, he would take care of me. He then ordered me to strip; when I refused he punched me hard in the face.'

At this point both Ah Gaik Chee and Ah Hwa Chee gasped in horror. Choo Choo Kor seemed to not have noticed their reaction, for she just continued on with her story.

'His punch must have knocked me out, when I regained consciousness he was on top of me and I felt incredible pain, there was blood everywhere. After he was done, he just got up and left me lying there on the small platform bed.'

'Did you know what had happened?' Ah Hwa Chee asked.

'No I didn't, I had no knowledge of sex, I did not understand what he had done to me', Choo Choo Kor replied. 'A few hours later seven Japanese soldiers entered the room. I started screaming when two of them grabbed my arms and one of them stuffed a rag into my mouth. Another two grabbed my legs and held them apart.'

This time Choo Choo Kor sobbed uncontrollably as she recalled the incident. Ah Gaik Chee, who was usually not a very touchy feely person, broke down and hugged her. This was the first time I actually saw Ah Gaik Chee hug anyone. Ah Hwa Chee just cried softly beside them.

'They, they...they took turns raping me, whenever I struggled they would punch me. The more I begged for them to stop the more they laughed. Whenever I struggled or screamed they would punch and kick me.'

'You don't have to continue if you don't want to, you don't have to tell us everything,' Ah Gaik Chee told Choo Choo Kor, but Choo Choo Kor insisted she felt better after talking about it. This secret had been eating inside of her for far too long, and she needed to tell someone.

'I was confused, tired, frightened, and in pain. I started to drift in and out of consciousness. Sometimes I felt like my spirit had left my body and I was just standing at the corner of the room, looking at what was happening. Each night five to seven soldiers would come and repeatedly rape me. They would sometimes burn me with an iron when I did not do what they want me to do,' continued Choo Choo Kor as she lifted her blouse to show them her scars from being tortured.

'Even when I fell ill from their continual raping and beatings, they did not take any pity on me.

'I had nightmares daily but when I awoke my reality was even scarier than my nightmares.

'My body was all torn up, I could no longer bear any children, I felt like I was no longer a woman, no man would ever want me as a wife.

'You know before all this happened, there was a boy that I liked and he liked me too, I believe. He was three years older than I was. His name was Yeoh Seng Guan.'

'What happened to him?' asked Ah Gaik Chee.

Choo Choo Kor looked down, as if ashamed. 'I don't know, all I knew was that I could never ever face him after what had happened to me. His parents would never allow him to marry a fallen woman.'

'Finally, after the war was over and I was released, I went home but life was no better. My parents, although they welcomed me home, could not hide the fact that they were ashamed of me.

'Whispers of me being a prostitute to the Japanese soldiers floated around until they could no longer take it.

'The vicious gossip just would not stop.' Choo Choo Kor's body was wracked with sobs again. 'My parents should have never been humiliated because of me.'

'I was thirteen then, I am sixty-three now, this nightmare just won't go away. At one time I wanted to hang myself, I truly did, but I was afraid...'

'It was a good thing you did not go through with it because people who die of unclean deaths like hanging become substitute-seeking ghosts,' Ah Gaik Chee interrupted.

'What do you mean?' Ah Hwa Chee asked.

'Well, firstly everyone knows if you commit suicide, you cannot be reborn, you will continue to suffer and relive the moment of your death over and over until you find a replacement. Also, secondly, you will have really bad karma because as a substitute-seeking ghost, the person that takes your place, you will, in turn, need to find someone else to take their place, and this cycle just goes on indefinitely.'

Choo Choo Kor nodded, agreeing with Ah Gaik Chee's explanation before continuing her story.

'Like I said, life was hard when I came back home. No one wanted to hire me because rumors had it that I had voluntarily collaborated with the Japanese. I was being paid by them to be a prostitute.'

Choo Choo Kor sighed then spoke again with anger and frustration in her voice, 'People believe what they want to believe. Why would a thirteen-year-old who have never even had sex, and don't even know what sex was, want to offer herself as a prostitute? Did they even stop to think about what they were accusing me of?'

'Anyway, after being taunted by their friends, neighbours and relatives, my parents decided that perhaps the best thing was to send me away. That was when they heard that a rich and prominent family was looking to adopt a young girl.'

'Was that the Lim family?' asked Ah Hwa Chee. Ah Gaik Chee rolled her eyes in exasperation before replying on Choo Choo Kor's behalf, 'Of course it was.'

'Did your parents not try to marry you off?' asked Ah Gaik Chee.

'No respectable family would want a girl that is no longer a virgin and no man would want a girl that can't give him children.

Because of what happened, my insides were all torn up. My womb had become so infected because of the repeated rapes. It had to be removed, so I couldn't ever have any children,' Choo Choo Kor explained in a soft voice, holding her head down in shame.

'If I had stayed on with my family I would only be a burden. Besides I have six other brothers and sisters that had to be taken care of. My parents were more than happy to let Lim Heng Soon's family adopt me. In a way, I was also happy to leave because my family would no longer have to live with the shame of what I had done. Heng Soon's family does not know my past, so please keep what I tell you tonight a secret.' Choo Choo Kor made both Ah Gaik Chee and Ah Hwa Chee promise. After that night it was evident that the three of them grew closer because they began to hang out together more often.

As for me, I felt terrible for how I had treated Choo Choo Kor. I vowed in my heart to treat Choo Choo Kor better in future and not fight with her so much, even when she spouted silly old wives' tales like young children should never eat chicken feet because it might mess up their handwriting skills when they start school.

Choo Choo Kor stayed with our family, serving us faithfully till the day she died, and me, I kept my promise to be kinder to her every day for the rest of her life.

# 11

# All for the Love of Red Bean Cookies

My friendship with Ah Hoon Cheh or Ham Cheem Peng Hoon Cheh started over some red bean cookies. She was one of the domestic servants hired to attend to my grandma and also expected to perform other miscellaneous chores around the house.

She was an unmarried older woman in her fifties. We gave her the nickname *Ham Cheem Peng* (Cantonese Fried Dough) because of her round doughy body and flat pancake-like face.

One of Ah Hoon Cheh's skills was making mouthwatering, delightful red bean cookies. I remember those early mornings when she would wash the beans and toss them into a huge metal pot. She would then boil the beans, and when they were cooked she would pour in the sugar and boil some more on low fire till the beans became mushy and turned a shade of darkish red or magenta.

While the beans were cooking in the pot, she would tell me to stay very quiet and listen to the beans telling us stories. She said if we remained really quiet, we could hear the adventures that the beans had gone through, stories of the sun and the skies and how the wind blew. I believed her and often squatted

quietly beside the metal pot, listening intently, but sad to say I never heard those beans talking.

Anyway, after the beans were thoroughly cooked to perfection, the paste was then placed in a flaky dough, rolled into tiny balls and baked in the oven. Geok Poh and I both loved these delicious melt-in-the-mouth cookies that were especially to die for when they were fresh from the oven.

Unfortunately, Ah Mah was very frugal with the distribution of these cookies. If she was in a good mood, she would give Geok Poh and me two each, saving the rest to impress any possible guests that might drop in to visit her during the week. So my cousin and I had to secretly devise a plan to increase our supply of those cookies.

'Maybe, we could steal some from her cupboard when she goes to the temple?' I suggested hopefully.

'No, she always counts them,' said Geok Poh in a thoughtful manner. 'Besides, her cupboard is always locked.'

'Charlie KoKo,' I suggested excitedly. 'He's always stealing stuff, maybe we can get him to pilfer some when they are fresh out of the oven.'

'No, I don't think so,' Geok Poh disagreed. 'If we get him to do it then our share would be less because he would want some too and we would have no choice but to give him some. Otherwise, I know, he would tell on us. If he doesn't tell on us, he would still use the information to blackmail us.'

'What about...'

'Keep quiet, let me think for a second,' Geok Poh shushed me impatiently. She was always better at this than me. She could be quite sneaky. Every time she wanted something she would send me to ask for it. If she wanted to go to the nearby shop to buy some munchies, she would send me in to ask for money. If she was thirsty for a bottle of F&N orange soda, which by the way was one of Tua Kor's rationed items, she would convince me that I wanted one too.

Once, Geok Poh convinced me to raid the kitchen pantry with her. It was the week before Chinese New Year and the pantry had just been stocked full of cakes and biscuits, including all my favourites: crisp 'love-letter' cookies, pineapple tarts, groundnut biscuits, flower-shaped butter cookies with a piece of cherry stuck in the middle, and rich, moist semolina cakes with chopped hazelnuts.

But how to enjoy these treats without anyone else finding out? Geok Poh had the brilliant idea to just eat the first layer of

biscuits in each tin and dispose of the thin paper that separated the first layer from the second. That way, it would appear as though the tins had been undisturbed. What a feast we had! And we got away with it too. That's why I trusted Geok Poh to come up with a good plan to get the red bean cookies.

Suddenly, Geok Poh snapped her fingers. 'Got it, why don't you make friends with Ham Cheem Peng Hoon?' suggested Geok Poh cunningly.

'What?' I exclaimed. 'Why?'

'Shhhhh, do you want the whole world to hear us?' Geok Poh spoke through clenched teeth.

'Because,' she rolled her eyes in exasperation, 'if that stupid woman thinks that we are her friends, we could persuade her to keep away some cookies for us. That way Ah Mah would never find out.'

'Why me? Why not you?' I asked incredulously.

'It's because she likes you better,' she said with conviction while looking at me from the corner of her eye.

'Okay, Okay,' I agreed grumpily, wondering what in the world I had in common with Ham Cheem Peng Hoon. We pinky swore not to tell anyone and the very next morning put our plan to work. So that's how my friendship with Ah Hoon Cheh started, based on greed, lies, and deception on my part, and ending with hurt, sadness, guilt and Ah Hoon Cheh almost losing her life.

The next morning I greeted Ah Hoon in a sickly sweet voice, 'Good morning, Ah Hoon Cheh, what are you doing, can I give you a hand?'

Ah Hoon Cheh looked at me, surprised. I usually ignored her unless there was something I wanted her to do for me.

'Nothing much, just washing some clothes,' replied Ah Hoon Cheh as she continued scrubbing her laundry. I stood there quietly watching her while searching my mind for something else to say.

'Maybe, I'll come back in the afternoon and help you take the clothes down from the clothesline,' I offered.

Ah Hoon Cheh just nodded absently without bothering to look up, continuing on with her task, not paying much attention to what I had said and not really expecting me to come back later. True to what she had predicted, absorbed with playing paper dolls with Geok Poh, I had completely forgotten my 'promise' to Ah Hoon Cheh until I heard the plip-plopping sound of raindrops hitting the roof.

As I ran outside, the wind and rain rushed upon me, whipping my cotton skirt against my legs and blowing drops of water across my face. Ah Hoon Cheh was already outside, battling with the clothes that were stiff and cold as corpses. I tried to pry the clothespins loose for her, but the clothes put up a fierce fight, beating my hands and face. Even after I had managed to get the clothespins loose, the clothes still hung on tight to the line with their death grips. Ah Hoon Cheh was forced to separate them one by one, very gently for fear of tearing them. By the time we had gathered them all, we were thoroughly soaked.

Ah Hoon Cheh muttered something that sounded like 'thanks' before hurrying me indoors. Horrified upon realizing that I was soaked to the skin, she immediately hustled me up to my room, where she stripped me, ran a hot bath for me, forced me to down a hot cup of Horlicks (my favourite malted milk drink) and tucked me in with a hot water bottle. I think she did all that out of fear rather than concern for me. If I had taken ill, for sure, she would be blamed for allowing me to help her.

After that day, Ham Cheem Peng Hoon Cheh treated me with less suspicion. Sticking to our plan to gain her trust, I set out to be friendly in unobtrusive ways. Things like finding Ah Hoon Cheh's slippers for her when Charlie hid them, sympathizing with her when she complained that her back ached or there was 'wind' in her bones, offering to get her a hot water bottle when she complained of a stomach ache. Just little things that I think not even Ah Hoon Cheh noticed at first.

Soon Ah Hoon Cheh's trust in me grew and she began to regard me as her friend, someone to be trusted. She even suggested that with Ah Mah's permission, she would like to take me to the wet market. I had always wanted to go to the wet market because I'd heard that it was a very exciting place with lots of things to see and buy.

After pleading with Ah Mah for a week, she finally agreed to let us go, provided Ah Gaik Chee went with us.

Geok Poh wasn't at all pleased with me spending so much time with Ah Hoon Cheh. She began to urge me to go to Stage Two of our plan, which was to convince Ah Hoon Cheh to bake her red bean cookies and save a batch for us. By now I was beginning to truly like Ah Hoon Cheh and was uncomfortable about following through with our plan, but I couldn't explain it to Geok Poh.

'You don't need to worry, Geok Poh,' I lied. 'I'm only using Ah Hoon Cheh. You know that, don't you? Why would I want a stupid old bat for a friend?'

So Geok Poh put up with my friendship with Ah Hoon Cheh. She even swallowed her irritation when Ah Hoon Cheh began to hang around us constantly interrupting our games by asking us what is this and what is that.

'I like that poly game, can get lots of money, buy hotels,' she exclaimed after our game of Monopoly.

'Teach me how to play,' she begged.

Geok Poh pursed her lips and her face turned as sour as a lemon.

'You don't know how to read, cannot play,' Geok Poh told her cruelly.

Ah Hoon Cheh looked at me for support but not wanting to anger Geok Poh, I averted her eyes and kept quiet. I knew if I looked at her I would feel guilty to see the hurt crawl over her face.

One day, something happened that put an end to this cruel game of deception and the tug of war between Geok Poh and Ah Hoon Cheh.

I woke up late one afternoon from a nap feeling unwell. My throat hurt especially when I swallowed and my eyes hurt when I moved them about. I had a cough too.

Ah Hoon Cheh looked at me with great concern, 'Do you feel alright? Here let me feel your palms.'

Upon feeling my hot palms she diagnosed that my body had too much heat and needed cooling down.

'Mung bean soup,' she prescribed with confidence. 'I'll go to the corner store and get you some.'

Ah Hoon Cheh's sense of direction and eyesight had always been bad. She couldn't even find her way home from the corner store in the morning, much less in the dark. But out of love for me, she put on her scarf and got ready to brave the dark unfamiliar street. She tried to persuade Cousin Ah Gaik to go with her, but Ah Gaik Chee was busy watching a Chinese soap opera and declined.

'I'll go with you after the show,' she offered knowing full well that the shops would be closed by then.

As Ah Hoon Cheh continued to get ready, Geok Poh stared at her in disbelief. 'Do you mean to tell me you are going to go all by yourself in the dark just to get Swee Lian some mung bean soup?' asked Geok Poh, her words coated with jealousy.

'Yes,' replied Ah Hoon Cheh in a quiet but determined voice. 'Swee Lian is sick and this is a small thing to do for a friend, she's been very nice to me.'

'Swee Lian isn't your friend,' sneered Geok Poh, as hatred overflowed from her heart and trickled like lava through her arteries.

'She is,' said Ah Hoon Cheh, with such certainty that Geok Poh became more irritated.

'Stupid old woman!' said Geok Poh scornfully. 'It was all part of our plan to use you. Don't you see that was the only way we could get you to secretly save a batch of red bean cookies for us?'

Poor Ah Hoon Cheh stood there her shoulders drooped like a weeping willow, purse still tightly clutched in her hand.

'You're making it up,' she said miserably, not daring to meet what she suspected would be Geok Poh's cold, triumphant eyes.

'It's true,' said Geok Poh spitefully. 'I tell you, we both planned it.'

I think Ah Hoon Cheh eventually believed her. No one could say such cruel words so emphatically if they weren't true.

'I am still going because I love Swee Lian. She's been kind to me,' said Ah Hoon Cheh in a stubborn but shaky voice as she walked out the backdoor.

'Stupid old hag!' mumbled Geok Poh under her breath.

She didn't tell me right away that Ah Hoon Cheh had gone off in the darkness to get me some mung bean soup. She was feeling a little ashamed for having been so outspoken. Besides, she was afraid I might be upset with her for letting the cat out of the bag regarding our 'plan' after we had both pinky sworn.

At 7.30 p.m., Tua Kor and Tua Tneow came home from visiting some friends, expecting dinner. But there was none.

'Ah Hoon, Ah Hoon ah,' shouted Tua Kor exasperated and hungry. 'Where's dinner?'

'Ah Hoon can be so irresponsible,' complained Tua Tneow. 'Couldn't she have prepared dinner before leaving?'

'I saw her about an hour ago,' said Cousin Ah Gaik, 'she said something about going somewhere, I'm sure she will be back in a minute'.

But five minutes, ten minutes, half an hour went by and there was still no sign of Ah Hoon Cheh.

By this time everyone was beginning to worry. Had something happened to her?

Geok Poh was in a dilemma, only she knew where Ah Hoon Cheh had gone. Surely Ah Hoon Cheh would be back soon— after all, she was only going to the corner store. But why was she so late, she should have been home half an hour ago. A cold hand crept around Geok Poh's heart and almost stopped her breathing. Suppose…suppose that Ah Hoon Cheh got knocked down by a car or even a reckless motorbike? Suppose that even now she is lying by the side of the road dead or badly injured! The thought was so terrible that Geok Poh suddenly felt sick.

Not knowing what to do, she came to me. I was starting to stir from my sleep disturbed by the commotion downstairs.

'Swee Lian, I must tell you something,' she whispered to me in a low and urgent voice. 'It's about Ah Hoon Cheh.'

I looked at her in alarm and nodded.

'What's the matter, Geok Poh?' I asked. 'You look like someone just died.'

'Ah Hoon Cheh went out to get you some mung bean soup at the corner shop and she never came back,' Geok Poh sobbed hysterically.

'Why didn't you stop her?' I asked angrily. 'You know how bad her eyesight and sense of direction is? How can you let her go out all by herself in the dark?'

'I tried to stop her, I even told her about our "plan" but she insisted that she loved you anyway,' said Geok Poh suddenly ashamed of herself.

'Oh, it's all my fault, we shouldn't have made that stupid plan,' I cried. 'I do love her, I didn't at first but now I do. And you sent her out thinking that I don't care about her. That I was just using her to get those stupid, stupid cookies.'

At that moment Tua Kor came in to find two very distraught girls, sobbing their hearts out helplessly by the foot of the bed.

'We found her. Poor Hoon, not being able to see very well, she took a wrong turn on her way home and stumbled into a storm drain.'

Geok Poh screamed. She shook Tua Kor's arm violently. 'Is she hurt? Is she badly hurt? You've got to tell us.'

'Yes, she was bleeding pretty badly, there was a deep gash on her head but luckily I think there were no broken bones,' said Tua Kor wiping her tears away but was a little puzzled at Geok Poh's reaction. She knew Geok Poh was not particularly close to Ah Hoon, so why the hysterical behaviour and sudden concern. Tua Kor wondered but was too preoccupied with Ah Hoon's condition to pursue the thought.

'Is she downstairs?' I asked, suddenly finding my voice.

'No, the ambulance took her away just a couple of minutes ago,' Tua Kor replied. 'Ah Gaik Chee went with them.'

A week passed before we heard any more news—a long, long week for both Geok Poh and me. So we were both excited when Tua Kor finally told us that she was going to take us to visit Ah Hoon Cheh.

We had to walk through a long corridor of beds before reaching Ah Hoon's at the very corner. Both Geok Poh and I wrinkled our nose at the strong smell of disinfectant and urine, but we didn't complain.

Suddenly we saw her lying in bed, still very pale. There was a big bandage on her head and bruises on her face, arms, and legs. My heart dropped when I saw her.

Upon seeing her, Geok Poh rushed over.

'I am so sorry, I said all those horrible things to you, please forgive me,' wailed Geok Poh. Ah Hoon Cheh patted her head and assured her that all was forgiven. She then looked over at me and started to apologize.

'Ai-yah Swee Lian ah, I am so sorry, I did not manage to get you the mung bean soup. The bag broke when I fell.'

I opened my mouth to tell her to forget about the soup, to tell her how sorry I am for being such a horrible person and that I truly do love her as both my friend and my aunt. But not one word came out. I gazed at her as if I could not look at her enough. And for the first time, I saw Ah Hoon's kind eyes, her hands that were calloused and roughen yet gentle, her heavily lined face full of compassion and I realized in that one minute how much she loved me and how much I loved her.

'I didn't mean to lie to you,' my eyes told her. 'I'm terribly sorry I hurt you. I will never be mean to you, ever again.'

Somehow Ah Hoon Cheh understood. She squeezed my hand and wiped my tears away.

'It's alright Lian,' she said, 'I know what you are feeling and thinking. No need to worry, all is forgiven.'

I think in everyone's life, there is that one person you wished you had been nicer to, that 'someone' who adores you no matter how mean you were to them, that 'someone' who is quick to forgive your mistakes, that 'someone' whom you had betrayed, that 'someone' you wished you had taken the time to get to know. For me, Ah Hoon Cheh was that person.

She left rather abruptly after this incident and to this day I have no idea what became of her.

# 12

# Cousin Geok Poh's Ghosts

Ghosts, evil spirits, deities, and mediums were a huge part of my life while growing up. But those were not the ghosts that I was most afraid of. It was Cousin Geok Poh's ghosts that really scared me, because nobody would believe her. Everyone acted like there was nothing wrong.

Geok Poh and I were very close, so I knew her behaviours fairly well.

According to my mother, Jee Kor and Uncle Harry adopted Geok Poh when she was only three years old. Like Choo Choo Kor, Geok Poh's family also sold her because they needed the money to feed her other brothers and sisters.

Her mother dropped her off at Grandma Cheah's house one day, telling her that she'd be back soon. Jee Kor then took Geok Poh to the courtyard at the back of the house and gave her a small twig, told she could use it to poke at some shy plants. Both she and I poked at the plant together and laughed gleefully as we watched its leaves close. Little did we suspect (not that either of us would have suspected, being just three years old) this was to enable Geok Poh's heartbroken mother, who was peeking out through the kitchen window, to catch one last glimpse of the daughter she was forced to sell to survive.

As soon as Geok Poh realized her mother was gone she began to cry. She would not stop crying because I guess she was scared. She was in a house full of people she didn't know and her mother was nowhere in sight. Since I was only a kid, I didn't remember much except that I suddenly had someone to play with. Geok Poh followed me around and parroted everything I did. She even called my mother 'mummy'. We were both inseparable, we did everything together.

Geok Poh was someone who was full of imagination and ideas, though sometimes I thought she took things too far. She loved scaring me and Mei Mei. I guess it gave her a sense of 'power' over us. One of the pranks she liked to play on us was pretending she was possessed. We would be playing some game and when I called her, she would turn around slowly and say in an expressionless voice, 'Geok Poh? Who is Geok Poh? She is not here.'

Because she was so full of imagination she was also really clever at telling stories... scary stories. One night as Mei Mei and I were getting ready for bed, waiting for our turn to use the bathroom to brush our teeth, Geok Poh suddenly ran out, shouting, 'It grabbed me, it grabbed me, I felt it grabbing me!'

Mei Mei and I rushed up to her. 'What grabbed you?' I asked fearfully.

'The hand that came up from the toilet,' replied Geok Poh as she glanced at the toilet bowl, her eyes full of fear.

That night regardless of how badly we needed to go pee, Mei Mei and I just held it in. When morning came, we both rushed into Tua Kor's room where she kept her personal chamber pot and relieved ourselves. For the longest time both Mei Mei and I always went to the toilet together, keeping each other's company. If the hand ever did come up to grab the one sitting on the toilet, at least the other could help pull her off the seat.

According to Geok Poh, there was also a creature that lived in the toilet. If either of us was to stay too long on the bowl, it would come up and bite our bums. When we were growing up, toilets were a scary place for both my sister and me because of Geok Poh's tales.

But I trusted Geok Poh with all my heart. I truly believed she was looking out for my sister and I. We were always very close growing up.

Then one day when Geok Poh and I were both fourteen, she changed. It started with her voice. It became as flat as a soda pop left open overnight. No excitement, no humour. Initially I thought that she was feeling sad because she had just broken up with Tony Goh Boon Eng, her very first boyfriend.

Well, he had never really been her boyfriend. I mean, we had only double-dated a couple of times. He would sometimes hang out at her place in the afternoon. I thought we were all just kind of 'dating around', nothing serious and I think Tony felt the same way because he also hung around other girls' houses, especially Lillian Ong, a girl from another school who always wore her skirts too short and her blouse unbuttoned too low. She lived down the street from us.

Geok Poh, however, was dead serious about their relationship. She fantasized a lot about him and would make up imaginary dates. I joined her because it was fun to dream about things we could do and would do and probably might do if we went on actual dates in the future.

Because Geok Poh took her relationship with Tony Goh seriously, she would often make 'boyfriend–girlfriend' demands on him. For instance, she wanted him to visit her at least four times a week in addition to their regular Saturday/Sunday dates and call her up to talk more after his visits were over. On days that he could not come, he was to call her up at least twice a day. She also felt that he should also bring her gifts like flowers and chocolates.

Tony never did any of those things but Geok Poh still insisted that she was his girlfriend. On days that she thought he would visit and never showed up, she would make up excuses for him and for the times that he said he might call and never did, she blamed the telephone company, saying the phone was probably out when he wanted to call.

As for the flowers and chocolates, well, I think he only gave her a rose once for her birthday. Geok Poh, however, managed to read a whole lot more into that one stem of rose.

'I think the red signifies the danger of our relationship,' Geok Poh whispered to me during one of our nightly chats. She and I both shared a room together with Ah Gaik Chee and Ah Hwa Chee. Our whisperings would usually start when we heard both of them snoring.

'What do you mean, danger?' I asked, not totally understanding her.

'Well, you know, if my mother or Tony's mother ever found out about our relationship, we would be in trouble,' she replied still staring up at the ceiling with unblinking eyes.

'Why?' I probed further.

'Because,' she replied in an exasperated voice, 'Mrs Goh once said she wanted to send Tony overseas to further his studies. Now that he is my boyfriend, how can he go?'

'The blooming petals are like our love, growing. And the fragrance is sweet like Tony,' she continued in a dreamy voice. 'You know he smells really good after his shower, I wonder what kind of soap he uses. I think he uses Old Spice, you know the soap on the rope kind.'

I did not respond as I had no idea what soap Tony used and I also did not know where she was going with all these. Suddenly her smile turned into a frown.

'The thorns. The thorns are his way of telling me that his mother is a thorn in our relationship. Oh, Swee Lian, what are we supposed to do?'

Again I made no reply as I was having trouble trying to digest her interpretations of the rose.

So you see, I really thought it was because of her sadness over the relationship that made her voice gone flat. If it was because of that then I wouldn't worry so much, since she'd get over it as time passes. Besides, no one else in the family seemed to notice the change in her, so I must have been mistaken.

With each passing day, Geok Poh began to act stranger and stranger. She would come home from school and begin to tell me situations that just didn't seem possible. Geok Poh and I went to the same school, and although we were in different classes, I knew half the girls that she was telling me about. She started by telling me that the girls in school were doing weird things. According to her, they used their hairstyles to communicate.

'Today Anne tied her hair up in a ponytail, so did May and Lynn,' she whispered as she pulled me into the corner of our small room. 'You know what that means? It means that they are indirectly telling me that they are better than I am, you know how the ponytail makes you look taller so that you can look down on another person?'

Not knowing what to say, I nodded in agreement trying to appear inconspicuous as I tugged hard on my own ponytail trying to stuff it into the back of my collar.

Through Geok Poh, I 'learned' the meanings of the different hairstyles. If your hair was braided, it meant you were trying to use it as a rope to strangle her. If the hair was cut short, it meant that the person had cut you out of her life. Curly hair signified a desire to mess with your brain making it all fuzzy and confusing. Two ponytails meant they were getting instructions from someone else. Although I never truly understood where she was coming from, I always took her seriously, never once laughing at the absurdity of her claims and interpretations.

As the months passed, Geok Poh got progressively weirder. There was one thing that puzzled me, her strange behaviour seemed to slip by everyone's attention. Nobody gave it a second thought. Even when she stopped coming down for her meals because her food tasted funny. She told me that she suspected

Choo Choo Kor had put something in it. Whenever they talked about her behaviour they spoke in a very nonchalant way.

'This Geok Poh is getting worse by the minute, so spoilt,' Ah Gaik Chee would say as if she were complaining about the weather.

'Yeah, I agree, I think she is doing this on purpose so that we have to serve her meals in her room,' agreed Choo Choo Kor, eager to please Ah Gaik Chee.

'Princess Geok Poh, who does she think she is?' Ah Gaik Chee would continue while casting a tentative glance at Geok Poh's solitary figure. At that moment, Geok Poh was standing by the doorway, talking to an unseen person.

'Let's just ignore her lah,' said Ah Hwa Chee heartlessly. 'The more attention we give her, the more she will act out.'

And so it seemed to be the consensus in the household that Geok Poh was just making trouble on purpose and seeking attention. When Geok Poh started laughing at inappropriate times, everyone complained that she was being rude on purpose.

'Aiyoh, this *char bor geena* simply laughs, this young girl ah very *boh kah si* so rude, can't she see that I am watching TV?' Ah Mah complained one afternoon when her favourite detective series *Columbo* was interrupted by Geok Poh's sudden explosive laughter.

In retrospect, I think everyone knew something was wrong, but they didn't know what and who was to blame, so everyone pretended that the elephant on the dining table did not exist. Even guests played along by acting like they did not notice Geok Poh's sudden laughter or her disjointed sentences or her obsession with her hands. No one dared say anything for fear of insulting the family.

Geok Poh's grades in school started to slip. Her normal As and Bs turned into Es and Fs. Teachers complained that she wasn't paying attention in school. They said she was always looking at her hands, complaining that they were different than they used to be. Sometimes she would just get up in the middle of a lesson and walk off. Later they would find her wandering aimlessly along the school corridors or in the girls' bathroom talking and laughing to herself. This made Jee Kor very mad at her. According to her, Geok Poh had just 'washed her dirty laundry in public.' Now it wasn't just a matter in the family. Other people were beginning to talk.

'You useless girl, waste my time and strength taking you as my child,' Jee Kor scolded while tugging Geok Poh by her ear.

'People are now laughing at us, saying that we have a mad girl in our house. People will think I am the one that drove you mad.'

'You shame the whole family, why are you doing this to me?'

Geok Poh didn't answer or protest. She just let Jee Kor yank her about like a lifeless puppet, pinching her until her arms and legs were covered with black and blue bruises.

During these episodes, Geok Poh would zone out, her eyes would be blank. No matter what Jee Kor did to her she didn't blink or change her expression. Soon Geok Poh began zoning out for long periods of time. This infuriated Jee Kor even more and she started to curse Geok Poh telling her that she should just leave the house and be a prostitute since she is of no use to the family.

At night when we were in bed I would try to console her by asking her if there was anything I could do. She would just shake her head and then start laughing in an eerie manner, stopping as suddenly as she had started. I don't know if Geok Poh became worse after Jee Kor's scolding and punishments, but I know she certainly didn't get any better. We even stopped going to parties and double dates because Geok Poh was sure that there were spies on the bus or that there was poison in her food and drinks. She kept saying that boys are only after one thing. Once they use you they discard you like yesterday's newspaper. Her remarks about boys made me wonder if Tony Goh had done something to her.

As time went by, things got worse. She began to pace all night long after barricading our bedroom door with furniture. Ah Gaik Chee, Ah Hwa Chee and I were deathly afraid of these episodes of hers but we did not dare say anything, fearing that we might get Geok Poh into more trouble. We certainly did not want her to be sent to Tanjung Rambutan, an asylum for the insane. My worry grew bigger because Geok Poh hardly slept now, but I didn't know whom to turn to. Nobody would believe me when I told them that something was wrong with Geok Poh.

One evening after dinner Geok Poh told me that everyone in the house except me had been replaced.

'Haven't you noticed that Tua Tneow's eyebrows are pointed upward and his ears are beginning to grow?' she asked me in a scared voice while stealing furtive glances at Tua Tneow, who was parked in his usual *por ee,* a cloth wooden deck chair, reading his newspapers.

She then slowly scanned the room and said, 'They all look smaller, haven't you noticed? That's how I know they've been replaced.'

'Sometimes, they replaced them with robotic gnome-like people who run around and pretended to be our family members.'

'They are all from another planet sent to destroy us. That's why we have to be very careful. The phones are bugged and the food may be poisoned. You are the only one I can trust.'

I looked at her and I would see fear, her eyes darting left and right like a scared rabbit, suspicious of every little movement. She also claimed the furniture seemed to be moving around on its own.

'You see even the furniture is taking a life of its own. They are restless because they know something is not right.'

'It's all been replaced so that they can monitor my every move,' she concluded sadly.

She said she knew all this because they told her. These people were sent to protect her. But sometimes they would tell her to do things that were bad. If she didn't obey them, they threatened to harm her. Once she told me that there was a lady voice that kept telling her to cut off her hair so that the others couldn't control her through the strands. Hair strands were like antennas ready to receive anything that was transmitted.

By now I was confused and frightened. Who were these people that she was talking about. Were they real or imaginary? Maybe they were lost spirits or ghosts? Hairs on the back of my neck stood up and a chill ran through my body as I entertained this thought.

One day after many many months since Geok Poh started to behave differently an idea struck me. 'Ghosts,' that's the answer, that's how I could get help for Geok Poh. That night Geok Poh wasn't the only one who stayed awake.

Early next morning, I acted terrified as I knocked urgently on Jee Kor's bedroom door.

'Geok Poh's possessed, Geok Poh's possessed,' I cried as Jee Kor opened her door.

'Last night I heard her talking in a foreign tongue to someone,' I whimpered. 'Maybe, maybe, the ghost that made

Charlie sick, came back and possessed Geok Poh. Maybe the ghosts were angry and decided to take revenge.'

This kind of talk my aunt and the whole family understood and accepted. Now they were ready to take action. Geok Poh was possessed. No fault of theirs. Nothing to do with their ancestral blood being tainted with 'madness' or the family's mistreatment of her. It was Geok Poh's own unlucky *oon-khee* (soul). It must have been low, meaning she was susceptible to evil spirits. Otherwise, how could the spirit have followed her home, they rationalized, so it was Geok Poh's own fault.

The very next day, Jee Kor, together with Tua Kor, took Geok Poh to a temple. At first Geok Poh refused to follow them, convinced that they were trying to lure her out of the sanctuary of her room and harm her. So they had to tell her that I was going too, and that they wanted to take us to a very special place. Upon hearing that I was going to be there, Geok Poh came out of the room and agreed to go.

The temple that we went to was different from the temple that Tua Kor took Charlie. Apparently the Taoist priests at this other temple were much more powerful, and were very adept at performing exorcisms. The temple was located at the very top of a hill that was shaped like a crane with its wings spread out. Ensconced in the front of the temple were the imposing statues of the 'Four Heavenly Kings'. Each king controlled one of the four points of the compass. As we approached the temple we could see the Giant of the North guarding the left side of the temple. He was enormous and fierce-looking, towering at least 10 feet tall. He held a reptile in one hand and a pearl in the other.

'Look,' Tua Kor pointed to the Heavenly King's reptile, 'this reptile will eat up anyone at his command. And do you see those two people trapped below his feet? Well, that's a murderer and a wicked person.'

Geok Poh and I looked silently at the figure and our eyes trailed down to the two small figures at his feet with mouth wide open in their silent screams, as Tua Kor continued to tell us about the Heavenly King that stood next to the Giant of the North.

'This one we call him the Guardian of the South.'

Geok Poh and I looked up and saw an equally fierce face looking down at us. Under his feet were a man and a woman with anguished expressions on their faces.

'Look at that umbrella,' Tua Kor explained to us, 'if he ever opened it, all the light in the world would be extinguished and the whole world would be plunged into darkness.'

'What about those two trampled under his feet, who are they?' I braved myself to ask albeit in a soft voice.

'He's trampling on a woman with low morals and a gambler,' she replied in a pious voice and proceeded on in a hurried manner.

'This other who carries a guitar is called the Guardian of the West. When he strummed, enemy camps would be burned down and harmony would be bestowed on the virtuous. The people under his feet are a drunkard and an opium smoker.'

Geok Poh wandered off before we could get to the last one. She seemed to be having an argument with someone that we could not see. Tua Kor and Jee Kor pretended not to notice, took off their shoes, and hurried inside the temple, sending me to get Geok Poh.

As we entered the temple, Tua Kor bought some joss sticks and candles for us to pray with. She even bought a bottle of oil, which we were instructed to pour into a large container with a floating wick in the middle. After praying, Jee Kor sought out the head priest, telling him about Geok Poh's plight. He gestured for us to follow him into a small incense-filled room at the back of the temple.

The room was dark and empty except for a table, a stool, and an altar, where a fierce-looking deity sat guarded by two tigers. There was a tape recording of some priests chanting 'NamoAmiToPhor' over and over. On the left side of the table there was a small plate of jasmine, in the middle, right in front of the deity, there was a container filled with smoldering joss sticks, and on the right hand side there was a stack of opaque yellow-coloured paper, a Chinese writing brush and red ink.

Geok Poh took all these in with an unexpected calmness at first. The head priest told us that the spiritual healer would be with us in a few minutes. Tua Kor and Jee Kor smiled at each other nervously. A couple of minutes before the healer came into the room, Geok Poh started pacing nervously. But before her mother or Tua Kor could say or do anything, the healer entered. He was a middle-aged man with a gaunt body and long skinny arms. His head was clean-shaven with three red dots imprinted on his forehead, just like a monk, but he wasn't wearing a monk's robe. He wore only a pair of loose brown cotton pants. The moment he entered the room Geok Poh began to rock and speak in a language we didn't understand.

A second man entered dressed in a white short-sleeve T-shirt and pants. He had a long white beard and looked rather stern but his manner was very pleasant. He explained to us that he was the interpreter, and the ceremony would soon begin.

The first man then straddled the stool and bathed himself in incense, then clasped his hands together on the table in prayer.

He bent his head down and seemed to be mumbling some kind of incantation. Suddenly, he began to nod and whirl his head in a violent manner, his eyes closed. His features looked as fierce as the Four Heavenly Kings that stood on guard outside the temple. My heart began to beat faster and faster, feeling like it would jump out of my body at any second. I stole a glance at my cousin, feeling glad that I wasn't the one seeking this person's help.

After suffering what looked like spasmodic convulsions, he started to speak in a spirit language. All the time the interpreter was standing calmly by the table awaiting instructions.

All of a sudden the fast movements stopped, the spiritual healer sat down with an unexpected grace and started talking in a woman's voice.

The interpreter looked toward Geok Poh and asked Jee Kor to move her over next to the altar table.

'This girl is surrounded by three different entities,' said the interpreter. Tua Kor and Jee Kor nodded.

'There is more than one dimension where both light and dark beings reside, do you understand? These entities are between the spirit and the ghost world.'

'Do you hear voices?' the spiritual healer asked in spirit language. Geok Poh nodded.

'Don't be afraid, you are blessed to live more in the spirit world than world of the suffering. Do you understand?'

'Two of the entities are people that you have wronged in your past lives. The third one is your guardian.'

'Because you don't know how to manage them, your soul is now in fragments. Do you understand me?'

'What can we do to heal her?' asked Jee Kor softly suddenly finding her voice.

The spiritual healer ignored her, he proceeded to pick up his writing brush, dipped it in red ink, took pieces of the opaque yellow-coloured strips of paper, and started writing.

'Put these leaflets above her bedroom door for seven days,' the translator told Jee Kor while pointing at Geok Poh.

The healer who was still frantically writing suddenly stopped and in his high feminine voice gave more instructions.

'These ones—' the healer held up a yellow piece of paper filled with red characters—'tell her to burn them and have her wash her body in the water filled with the ashes and petals from seven different kinds of flowers.'

The healer then fainted and had to be shaken awake. My aunts murmured their thanks and hastily retreated from the room.

We were all very quiet on our bus ride to home. No one wanted to discuss what had happened. When we arrived home, Jee Kor did as the healer instructed.

Several days later, everyone said that Geok Poh's condition was much improved. But I knew better. Despite the best efforts of her family and the healer, Geok Poh was never quite the same. I felt like I had lost her that day, and our friendship never recovered.

# 13

# Blessed Water, Ghost Child and Fortune Tellers

As I grew older, probably around age sixteen, I began to be just a tad skeptical of these superstitious 'warnings.' Nevertheless, I still followed the 'rules' just in case. Hey, if someone told you that by drinking some blessed water you could get higher grades, you would drink it, wouldn't you? That's exactly what I did. I drank till my bladder pleaded for mercy, especially when I hadn't studied for the exam. My grades didn't improve, but I continued drinking the 'blessed water' before all my exams.

Apart from trying to improve my grades by drinking blessed water, my obsession with finding the 'right' man also grew. Gone were my childish days of consulting the spirit of the coin; I now resorted to more 'sophisticated' methods. My older cousin, Ah Hwa Chee, frequented fortune-tellers every other week or so just in case her fortune were to change in the course of that week. She was kind enough to let me tag along and learn. She strongly believed in fate or predestination. She also believed in luck and had resorted to a variety of ways to avoid bad luck and increase her wealth and prosperity. However, her deepest desire was to secure a husband for herself and live a happy life.

In order to find out about future prospective husbands she would also seek out the oldest known method of fortune-telling in the world, which is known as Thiew Chiam or Kau Chime.

'Now listen to me carefully, when I start shaking the container of bamboo stick, you will remain very quiet as not to disturb my concentration, do you understand?' Ah Hwa Chee asked as she looked at me seriously.

I nodded. 'Yes, I understand. Is it ok if I prayed in my heart too?' Her lips broke into a tiny smile and she said, 'Yes, of course.'

Ah Hwa Chee then held the container in both her hands and shook it vigorously until one of the sticks eventually rose and fell out. Watching that one single stick rise and then fall out of the container as if by some magical force was very exciting to me. I wanted to clap my hands, but decided against it. After all, we were in a temple and I don't think that would be an appropriate behaviour.

As Hwa Chee picked up the stick from the floor, she motioned to me to come closer and whispered in my ear, 'Swee Lian, I forgot to pick up the *puay*, can you go over to that corner table where the joss sticks are and pick them for me?'

'What do they look like?'

'You see over there? Those red things, shaped like half circles, one side round and the other side flat?' She pointed to the table. Very reluctantly I walked across the temple hall and picked up the two moon-shaped blocks.

As I was handing them over to her she motioned for me to sit beside her again.

'Hurry, sit, sit, let's get this over with,' she said as she held the two blocks inside the palm of both her hands and made a praying motion. Her hands moved up and down a few times before she opened them and let the blocks drop to the ground.

'Aiya, two of the flat sides are facing up, that means Kwan Yin is laughing at me,' she explained to me.

'Oh,' I said quietly, not really sure how to respond. She continued to repeat the first step again, praying with both blocks clasped in her palms. This time when she dropped the block it landed with one rounded side up, and one flat side up.

'Ahh good, good, confirm this is the stick,' my cousin sighed with relief.

The stick was then taken to one of the caretakers of the temple, the number on the stick was cross-referenced with ancient texts (or so I believed at that time), and her fortune would be told. The fortune is generally a short poem or rhyme, and the point is not so much to have a clear picture of her future but rather an indication of the possibilities, which lies ahead.

'Thanks Ah Hwa Chee for bringing me,' I said, thinking to myself this was something that might be useful in the future in case I have questions of my own.

My aunts, on the other hand, had more sophisticated methods of finding out about their future. According to my aunts, the face could be used to tell the future and fortune of an individual.

I had an aunt who we called Kah Leng Ee, 'Auntie Myna Bird.' I think she was given this nickname because she was small and stocky like a myna bird. She was also quite messy especially when she ate, and mynas are known for being very messy birds.

Anyway, Kah Leng Ee was very good at this type of fortune-telling. Whenever she came to visit, we would all gather around her and watch in fascination as she told fortunes just by looking at the shape of all the major features of your face.

One Saturday morning during one of her visits, I watched as she sat in the kitchen, dunking her Chinese doughnut into her black coffee and spilling droplets of it as she raised it to her mouth while telling the fortune of Mr Yong, one of our neighbours.

'Do you know there are ten facial types in total?' she asked Mr Yong while staring at him intently as if to establish her authority on the subject.

'No, I didn't,' Mr Yong answered, like a school boy being questioned by his teacher.

'Well there is, the ten facial types are *feng, mu, shen, tian, tong, wang, jia, yang, yuan,* and *you.* Each facial type is believed to have its own fate characteristics,' Kah Leng Ee continued.

'You, Mr Yong, hmmm...you have *mu* features. You have a lot of intelligence but you have bad gambling luck.'

Mr Yong looked upset as if my aunt had put a curse on him or something, he stood up in anger, kicked his stool aside, paid Kah Leng Ee and left. My aunt wasn't the least bit affected by his behaviour. She just shrugged and called after him, 'I just tell what I see, I did not make your face.'

The third and most easily accessible method of fortune-telling was palm-reading. When I was growing up, palm readers could be found at every corner in every street. I think having one's fortune told is more an indication of the conditions ahead rather than actual events. The opportunity, therefore, exists for people to make the most of their lives by being more aware of the 'environmental conditions' which surround their lives.

To find a prospective husband, single ladies would normally seek the help of a fortune teller. However, when their husbands strayed, they would resort to seeking out a deity for help.

One night as I was going down to the kitchen for a glass of water, I chance upon a conversation between my older cousin and one of her married friends.

'Don't worry, we can consult a bomoh, I know a good shaman and he will guide you on how to win your husband back from the other woman,' whispered Cousin Gaik confidently to her sobbing friend.

'If need be, we can *hae guan* (make a vow or promise to the deity). This is how it normally works, once you place a vow and your wish is fulfilled, you will need to visit the deity with some offerings such as nasi kunyit, flowers, fruits, and sireh leaves, etc. to say thanks.'

I am unsure what the outcome was because my cousin's friend seldom came around after that.

While my relatives had their own way of seeking guidance—from using different methods of fortune tellers, to placing vows with deities, kauchimes, face reading, and palm reading—to find answers for whatever life problems they may be facing, my parents turned to darker spirits for help.

If you remember, earlier on I had told you that I was sure that my dad was happy with me being a girl. Well, when this one incident happened, I began to have my doubts. Perhaps he had wanted a son. Perhaps my Da had in fact wanted a son but could not bring himself to admit it, so he and my ma used this as an excuse.

One Saturday morning, at the beginning of our long school holidays in the month of November, Da came home with a surprise for us.

'Swee Lian, Swee Ling, come downstairs, I have a surprise for you,' he yelled as he entered the house. 'Tell your Ma to come out too.'

'What's all the excitement about Jimmy?' my Ma yelled from the kitchen. 'I'm in the middle of cooking lunch.'

'Just come for a quick second,' replied my Da with a twinkle in his eye.

Mei Mei and I were already downstairs, thinking he had bought home some goodies for us to eat. That's what Da normally did when he came home. He would surprise us with different foods such as spring rolls or red bean-shaved iced or curry puffs, our favourite savoury pastry.

Ma finally emerged from the kitchen wiping sweat from her brow she looked at Da hoping he would quickly explain what he was so excited about.

'Ling.' That's what he called Ma, short for darling.

'Ling, remember you have been wanting to visit your favourite aunt who lives in Thailand?'

Ma looked at Da, not really sure where he was going with this. 'Yes,' she finally replied, 'the one who lives in Danok?'

'Guess what, I contacted her and her husband and we are going to take a road trip to visit her,' Da said happily. 'We will be staying with them for two weeks. A sort of mini vacation, I know you have not seen her for a long time so. . . surpriseeeeee!!'

Ma's face lit up with a smile.

Mei Mei just jumped up and down yelping like a puppy, 'Yaay yaay yaay, we are going on a holiday!'

As for me, I wasn't too excited about it. I loved my Kor Poh Gelap (that was her nickname, which meant 'dark skinned grandaunt') and I wanted to see her, but I was not all that keen on going to Thailand, a land of spirits, ghosts, black magic, and demons.

My grandaunt had married a Thai national, and that was why she lived in Thailand. I remember when I was about seven years old, we went there for a visit. I did not like it at all. I remember being scared most of the time. My aunt's house was a wooden house on stilts and had an attap roof. It was dingy and dark, smelt musty, and was supposedly haunted, but my parents did not care because according to my dad, we had enough amulets with us to fend off any evil spirits.

Da had already decided we would go, and I knew my Ma wanted to see her aunt, so I did not put up a fight about going. Besides, Mei Mei was really happy we were going on an actual holiday. Not being very well-to-do, we seldom went on long holidays away from home.

Mostly my Da took us for picnics by the beach or waterfall. We loved those outings because either for our lunch or tea, depending on what time our trips were, Ma would pack packets of delicious economy *char bihun*. To me these fried rice vermicelli noodles were the best because of their simplicity. They were just basic vermicelli fried in some chopped garlic, vegetable oil, light soy sauce, with a dash of salt and white pepper, a teaspoon of fish sauce and a tablespoon of dark soy sauce for colouring. The only vegetable in it would be bean sprouts, the only vegetable that I didn't hate. Oh, so simple, yet so tasty.

Without fail, along the way we would also stop to buy our favourite picnic snacks which was *goreng pisang* (deep fried banana fritters), deep fried sweet potatoes and if we were lucky, deep fried chempedak fritters when they were in season. Yippee. The best thing about these fried chempedaks was that even the seeds could be eaten, yum, yum. For drinks we would buy packets of freshly squeezed sugar cane juice that taste so good even without ice.

Another activity that we especially loved when we were at the beach was digging for *siput remis,* a kind of shellfish. These mini clam-like creatures can be found in abundance on the sandy shores of Penang Island. It would normally take an hour or two of digging before our buckets were full. We would then bring them home and Ma would stir-fry them with some black soya sauce, ginger and sugar.

Anyway back to our Thailand trip, upon entering the house, I felt uneasy, but I did not voice my feelings because I did not want to upset the family. Every room in the house was dark, and there were strange altars with figurines and objects everywhere.

'Come, come eat up, I have prepared all your favourite Thai food,' said my grandaunt to my mom as she invited us to sit down for dinner.

I looked at the food tentatively, as I did not like spicy foods and most of the dishes seemed to be loaded with just vegetables.

'Eat Swee Lian, your Kor Poh spent the whole day cooking for us,' my mother said in a tone that was laced with an unspoken warning for me to just eat and not make a fuss.

I picked up a piece of what I thought was chicken and ate in silence. My eyes wandered to the corner of the room, where there was a small doll sitting on a wooden stool. Unable to contain my curiosity, I asked my aunt, 'Kor Poh, is that doll for me?' thinking perhaps she had bought it for me as a present.

My grandaunt was silent for a moment before looking me straight in the eye and replied in a serious tone, 'That is not a doll, it is my child.' I looked at my mom, as I was unable to comprehend what Kor Poh meant by that. Ma just casually kept eating her dinner and dished out more chicken for me.

'Faster, eat before your rice becomes cold,' was all she said.

That night before bedtime, my Kor Poh came in to tuck me in and kiss me goodnight. She sat at the edge of my bed and began patting my back in a loving manner.

'Swee Lian ah, earlier I did not mean to reply you so sternly, it's just that those are not dolls for children to play with. These dolls have spirits in them,' she explained patiently.

Apparently, the doll in my grandaunt's house, the one I had wanted to play with, had the spirit of a 'ghost child' that my grandaunt had adopted.

Little did I know that that was also the reason why our family was there. My parents somehow got into their heads that in order to help them with their relationship and financial situation, they wanted to adopt a ghost child.

My Kor Poh explained to me that ghost children are usually the spirits of unborn babies that had died inside their mothers' wombs.

'Normally a priest or monk would dig out the body of the dead mother—' she paused for a second, picked up a sunflower seed, bit on it to crack open the shell, and used her tongue to flick the flesh into her mouth—'cut out the unborn baby from her, perform some rituals and then bake the baby into a figurine or amulet figure.'

I caught my breath and felt a chill run down my spine but made no comment.

I was just a child—till today I can't quite fathom why my Kor Poh would deem it appropriate to go into such gory details when she explained it to me. After her explanation about her newly adopted doll child, I felt even worse. To begin with I had already disliked staying at her house because it was always so dark and there seemed to be shadows lurking everywhere. I stayed awake for hours that first night.

The second night, as I was preparing for bed, it felt ominous again. I can't quite pinpoint what made me afraid to close my eyes, but I must have fallen asleep because the next thing I knew, I felt sharp painful tugs. My hair was being pulled. When I looked up, I saw little people, tiny dark figures almost like fairies, except they had sharp white teeth that gleamed.

'It's a dream, it's a dream,' I chanted and tried to take deep breaths to calm myself down. I tried to sit up but couldn't. I tried to call out and wake my parents up but somehow I could not, I opened my mouth and tried to scream but I was incapable of producing any sounds, my voice remained soundlessly inside my body, nothing came out.

I lay there stiffly on my back, catching a glimpse of my parents out of the corners of my eyes, fast asleep, seemingly oblivious to what was happening to me. I tried to reach out and tug on Mei Mei's pajamas, maybe that will wake her up. She was sleeping soundly just mere inches beside me but I was unable to move my arms or legs. I felt paralyzed. Not being able to shout or move, I did the only thing I could which was to silently chant in my heart '*Namo Kwan Say Im Phor Sat.*' I called out to the

Goddess of Mercy over and over and over again, begging her to come protect me. I am not sure if she heard my cries, but after a while the tugging stopped. My pajamas were soaked in sweat, but at least I could slowly move again. I wiggled my fingers, then my toes, then slowly propped myself up into a seated position. I eventually fell asleep hugging a bolster tightly for protection, my back against the wall, the remaining pillows forming a 'fort' around me.

'Are you sure you want one in your house?' I overheard my grandaunt asking my parents early the next morning when they thought I was still asleep.

Both my mother and father nodded. My Ma explained, 'The reason we need it is because times are hard now, the economy is not doing well, our business is dwindling, people prefer to buy from larger companies.'

'Yes, financially we are not doing well, some of it is due to my gambling habit,' my father admitted, his head bowed low. He then continued in a soft voice, 'This lack of finances is also affecting our relationship, we are constantly quarrelling.'

'Okay, if you are sure,' my grandaunt confirmed. 'The reason I am asking is because normally it is not advisable for a family who already has children to adopt a ghost child. Sometimes the ghost child might become jealous and harm the child,' she explained further.

I guessed my parents must have been desperate because in spite of the warning, they proceeded to adopt the ghost child.

The one my parents took home with us looked like a very, very small child. I was told that this was my younger brother, Didi. We all treated the doll like an actual family member. My parents treated him like he was their own son and often refer to themselves as 'papa and mama' whenever they spoke to him.

'Didi, you are a good boy today, mama will give you a hug before you sleep,' said Ma in a cooing voice whenever Didi behaved himself. It was strange to hear her speak in such a loving and soft manner to him because she never spoke that way to Mei Mei and me.

'Yes Didi, I will buy you a comic book and a ball tomorrow,' said Da as he stroked the doll's hair and patted its head.

Each night after dinner we would place sweets and chocolates out for my little brother, if it was hard candy, we would need to change it once the sweets or chocolates turned soft. Didi especially liked red-coloured drinks, so sometimes Ma would give him strawberry-flavoured Fanta. I felt jealous because my sister and I hardly ever get to drink fizzy drinks except for special occasions or festive seasons such as someone's wedding or Chinese New Year. Sometimes I felt that my little 'brother' was better fed than I was, even his milk had to be fresh each day with a drop of my parents' blood in it.

My brother was a very mischievous spirit. He was not evil like some others, but he liked to play tricks on me, often hiding my things or breaking my belongings. But Ma and Da seldom believed that it was him; often when things went wrong I was the one they would blame. I secretly thought they might be afraid of him.

One day a little after midnight, I was awakened by the sound of sobbing next to my bed. I awoke to see my little 'brother' doll, next to me. I was not afraid but I could sense that the doll appeared to be. I am not sure if once again I had been dreaming and this was just another nightmare, but somehow I could feel his fear. Inexplicably, he somehow managed to communicate to me through my mind.

'Cheh—' that's what he called me, referring to me as his elder sister— 'Cheh, there is another spirit in our house, it is black and it crawls on all four legs.'

I could feel his fear as if it were my own. Apparently, the creature had been tormenting my brother by biting and scratching him.

Strange that he should mention this creature because many times I thought I had seen something black and hairy scurrying across the floor or up the wall, hidden in the shadows but I chalked it up to my imagination. Could this be the same creature that I had seen during the exorcism of the teenage boy at the temple? Did it follow me home? No, I don't think so, it must have been my imagination, after all who would believe me if I told them my doll brother spoke telepathically to me.

Didi was with us for only a year.

All I knew was that after frequent complaints from Ah Mah expressing her unhappiness over our little 'brother', my Da decided he would take it to the nearest Thai temple and asked if they could take him. I am not sure if they did, but one day I came home from school and my brother was no longer there. I tried asking Ma about it but all she said was, 'Kids should not ask too many questions, none of your concern. This is adult matter.'

To me it seemed strange that my grandma did not approve of Didi. She herself subscribed to many outdated customs and traditions which included a multitude of superstitious beliefs. Anyway, she was the matriarch and we lived under her roof, so we had to abide by her rules whether we agreed with them or not.

Since we are talking about my grandma, let me share with you a little about my Ah Mah and her beliefs. Ah Mah was very particular about time. As a child I could never understand why she got so upset whenever there was a delay during certain events. Especially when it came to religious rites, she was very rigid and insisted that they must always be performed within the appointed time or hour; otherwise 'chiong' (clashing of the souls) might occur.

Ah Mah also consulted the Chinese Almanac regularly to determine the day and time for different events. For instance, during my aunts and my parent's wedding, Ah Mah used the almanac to determine what day the wedding should be, what time the bride should be picked up along, with numerous other wedding rituals.

One of these rituals that she had always insisted on was that whoever the bride was, may it be my aunts or my mom, on their wedding day they always had to wear a Phoenix collar over their wedding gowns. This collar was an embroidered multilayered mini shawl that has many movable layers which represented the beautiful feathers of a phoenix, and it was believed to protect the bride from evil spirits. The long tassels and ribbons which dangled down the back also had small reflecting mirrors hanging facing away from the bride, protecting her from demons.

Another thing that Ah Mah was very particular about was gifts. I remember one year during her birthday she got really upset because someone gave her a watch as a gift.

'Aiyo, aiyo,' lamented my grandma. 'Why did Ah Huat Ko give me a watch? Does he want me to die? Is he telling me my time's up?'

My Ah Kong tried to calm her down by offering to return the gift back to his brother, Ah Huat Ko.

'Don't be too upset, I am sure he is just being ignorant. I will return the watch back to him tomorrow.'

'What will you tell him?' asked my Ah Mah. 'I don't want him to think I look down upon his gift.'

'Leave it to me,' said Ah Kong in his usual loving voice. 'Let's just enjoy the rest of your birthday. Come, come eat your mee suah.' He took her by the arm and led her to the dining table where there was a bowl of steaming hot thread noodle soup. Eating mee suah is eating birthday cake for the Hokkien people—it symbolizes a good long life for the birthday person.

Just as I thought everything was fine, after her meal, someone suggested Ah Mah, Mei Mei and I take a picture together. She got upset again and absolutely refused. Mei Mei and I were baffled, why didn't Ah Mah want her picture taken with us. She then later explained that if three people took a photograph together, the one in the centre would be the first to die.

My Ah Mah also loved things in identical pairs. She had two identical lanterns hanging on the front porch of her house, in her bedroom there were two identical oil lamps, and on the altar there were two identical vases, one on each side of her deities.

Oh and one more thing, of the deities that she worshipped who sat on the main altar table, there had to be three and not two. According to Ah Mah, if there were only two deities on the altar and they should quarrel, there would be no one there to arbitrate.

One other superstition that Ah Mah subscribed to was that we were forbidden to sleep with our feet pointing towards the door, for she believed that this was the 'death position.'

Apart from her many superstitions, Ah Mah during her later years also taught us many of our childhood games. Most of these games were sedentary so she did not have to move around. Two games that particularly stuck in my mind were *Injit Injit semut* and Hot Wok.

*'Injit Injit Semut Siapa Sakit Naik Atas'* is a song we would chant while playing this game. I am not sure what 'Injit' means but I think the whole chorus just means being bitten by ants, whoever feels pain go to the top. You see, this is a pinching game. Geok Poh, myself, Mei Mei, and Ah Mah would stack our hands on top of each other, pinching the hand that was directly beneath ours. Then we started chanting the song over and over and the hand at the bottom would go up to the top.

The next game was a more exciting one. Ah Mah would pretend that the palm of her hand was a wok. She would pretend to wash it with her other hand while chanting *'say thnia, say thnia'* meaning 'wash pan, wash pan,' and then she would pretend to pour oil into her palm, *'hae ewe, hae ewe.'* We would each put our finger in the middle of her palm (wok) barely touching and asked *'Ewe sek ow boey,'* (Is the oil hot?)? We would ask that over and over, not knowing when she would say *'sek liao'* meaning 'oil is hot,' while simultaneously closing her palms and catching whoever was too slow in removing their fingers.

We would spend hours playing that game with her, and at the end of these sessions she would often reward us with a 20-cent coin. We were always very happy when she did that, and would take the money to an old sundry shop located at the corner of the road, spending it on treats like a bottle of Fanta grape or F&N Sarsi, Apollo chocolate wafers, or bubble gum and splitting our buys.

If it was raining and we could not go out, we would wait for the sound of *tok tok mee* man to come around so we could spend our reward. The tok tok mee man sold his noodles from a pushcart which he pushed around the neighborhood while knocking on his slab of bamboo with a stick to announce his presence.

I was told that if we listened carefully we could tell by the sound of his tok tok what type of noodles he was selling on that particular day. If it was the dry wonton noodles the sound would be a straight beat, tok tok tok tok tok. If it was fishball noodles, the sound would alternate between a high and a low pitch. As kids we never really paid much attention—the moment we heard the tok tok sound we would rush to find either Ah Gaik Chee or Ah Hwa Chee and ask them to help us out. We hardly ever ordered the fish noodles because the three of us, myself, Geok Poh and Mei Mei, preferred the wonton egg noodles.

Since we could only afford a bowl, we usually shared between the three of us. Squatting behind the back of the house where the laundry was usually done, we would take turns eating the warm springy egg noodles coated in special soya sauce, making sure to evenly split the char siu (barbeque pork) and the bite-sized wontons. Nobody really wanted the *chai sim*, so the leafy vegetables were usually left behind.

Those were some of my fondest memories of my grandmother. I may not understand many of my Ah Mah's superstitious beliefs, and I may have grumbled at the restrictions she often placed on us that made absolutely no sense to me, but nevertheless I know deep in my heart that she held on to those beliefs to protect her family. She even went to the extent of prohibiting utterances that are associated with death, believing that they might be prophetic.

# 14

# Paper Servants, Black Cats and, Cardboard Chauffeurs

When I was seventeen, my paternal grandfather passed away. It was a sad yet strangely exciting time for me. We'd never had a death in the family, and since he had been bed-ridden for some months now, we were 'prepared' for the inevitable.

I remember coming home from school and seeing my grandfather's body being laid out in the main hall on a long bench behind a white cloth. My heart felt a squeeze and tears welled up in my eyes, but I choked it down. I know I said we were 'prepared,' but to actually see him lying there motionless, reality suddenly struck that he was truly gone.

A Taoist priest was called to bathe him and clean him up. Before putting Ah Kong's body into the coffin, the priest asked, 'Where is his eldest son?'

My Da who had been standing on the side, stepped forward.

'Come, come closer,' instructed the priest. 'You need to feed rice to your father before we place him in the coffin.'

Ah Mah seemed very calm as she looked lovingly at Ah Kong's body being prepared, but I could see that her eyes were red rimmed and puffy.

'Here.' She handed the priest Ah Kong's spectacles and his favourite harmonica. 'He needs his glasses to read the newspaper every morning and when he is bored he can play his harmonica.'

The priest placed the two special items in the coffin and turned to Ah Mah. 'Anything else?' he asked.

Tua Kor, who was standing beside Ah Mah with tears streaming down her cheeks, sobbed as she handed a book to the priest, 'This was my dad's favourite book of poems, he can read them whenever he has time.'

Ah Mah suddenly cried out, 'His *cheo thau* garments, his wedding eve initiation garments, we need to put those on him. He needs to wear them, he needs to wear them.' She looked around panic stricken, her eyes scanning, searching for the white garments that Ah Kong had worn during his coming-of-age ceremony before their actual wedding began.

Jee Kor and Tua Kor, put their arms around her and tried to console her. 'It's all here Ah Mak, it's all here, we were about to ask the priest to put that on him,' Jee Kor said as she handed the garments to my grandma. 'Don't worry, we have not forgotten.'

'Why are the garments so important?' I asked my Ma in a low voice.

'Because the garments are made on the same day and time, it is believed that the wedding-eve clothing worn by both the bride and groom will enable the deceased to locate each other in the afterlife,' Ma explained to me.

Ah Kong looked peaceful as he lay there in his white suit as if in a deep sleep. A pearl wrapped in betel leaf was placed in his mouth to prevent him from coming alive and talking.

The body was kept in an open casket for the next seven days. My grandma had instructed all mirrors in the house and any reflective surfaces to be covered with cloth. It was believed that if the deceased were to catch their own reflection in the mirror, they would become a ghost. Household deities, on the other hand, were covered with red paper so that they would not get defiled by the death in the family.

'Choo Choo, remember your job is to sit beside the coffin,' instructed Ah Mah, 'we don't want any black cats to hop over it'

'Why?' I asked.

'Well, if a cat hops over the coffin the corpse will sit up and come back to life,' explained my Ah Mah patiently as if explaining some scientific fact to me.

There were also other important rituals that we had to observe for the next seven days. The *cucu cicit*—grandkids were put on 'duty' to make sure that the incense offerings do not burn out. Food was also offered to Ah Kong during all mealtimes to make sure that he did not go hungry.

Another excitement (for us kids at least) was changing into black clothes, which we were required to wear for forty-nine days. I am not exactly sure why we were excited about this but I guess wearing all black seemed cool and made us different from other non-mourning kids.

For the next seven days, various friends and relatives came and paid their respects. Another ritual that seemed strange to me was how people were expected to pay their respects to the deceased.

One day, I am not sure which day it was, I just remembered it being an afternoon, when one of my distant aunts came to pay her respects. Upon arrival she was cheerfully talking and laughing and shaking hands with people but the moment she stepped into the house, she wailed loudly by my grandfather's coffin.

'Ah Thneow ahhhhhhhh, *hamisu hamisu*, why, why, why did you have to go so young? Why did you not wait for me to come visit you one last time,' she wailed loudly. She continued wailing as I stood and watched fascinated with her obvious display.

There were no tears but she kept on for a good five–ten minutes, lamenting how my grandfather could no longer be with her and that my grandpa was not supposed to leave this world so soon, and so on.

As suddenly as it started, the wailing stopped, she stood up as if nothing had happened and came out to rejoin the group in cheerful spirits.

I thought it was so strange until later on I found out that loud wailings were compulsory, as they demonstrated that the deceased was much loved and would be missed. In fact, there are people who are hired as professional mourners in some cultures. There were a number of reasons why a family would want to hire a professional mourner (*hao lam*): perhaps they were embarrassed by low attendance, or perhaps they wanted to make the deceased seem more popular and important. Or if, for some reason, no one showed up for the funeral (and most cultures believe that the deceased was still 'hanging around') then the lack of attendance might make him or her really sad.

Imagine if you are dead and hovering around your casket and no one is crying that you are gone, no one shows that they are going to miss you, no one sitting and telling stories about how good a person you were. That scene can be pretty depressing. After all, it is your final farewell, you should have a happy send off. Overall, in case of any of the above reasons, I believe that the decision comes from a good place.

The following are my memories of the next seven days. Not entirely sure they are accurate but this was how I remember it. There was food all day long, cooks were hired to cook, bak moey (minced pork porridge) for the guests, there were rice dishes for dinner and then there were afternoon tea desserts served to guests who dropped by to pay their respects. There was also non-stop chanting, Siamese priests, Ceylonese priests, Taoist priests, all of them took turns chanting Buddhist scriptures each day to ease the journey of my deceased grandfather into the other realm.

During the funeral, as the coffin was being nailed shut, we were instructed to cry and grieve as loudly as possible. Then we were all instructed to turn away from the coffin as it was being sealed because apparently it was a taboo to watch. Till this day I have no idea why. Some people speculate that just before the coffin is sealed, the people who are in charge of the funeral rites will quickly steal all the jewellery and anything of value that the family has put into the coffin, but I choose to believe they do no such thing. After the coffin is sealed, yellow and white paper, apparently 'hell money,' was affixed to the surface of the coffin, then more prayers were said.

Before the casket is taken out, we were ordered to turn away one more time while it was being loaded onto the hearse. Then the family walked behind the hearse for a little distance before we got into the car and drove to the funeral parlor.

The following events may not be very accurate for it has been so long since my Ah Kong's funeral. However, I do remember that people also entertained themselves by gambling, especially when they kept vigil at night. In addition, there was always plenty of food being served to guests who attended the wake.

One dessert that stuck out in my mind was the black sweet glutinous dumplings called or bee koh that we served to the pallbearers during the ritual to keep them from being hungry. This dessert was soft, sweet, and sticky.

'Swee Lian, take this plate of bee koh, make sure they each take only a piece otherwise there would not be enough for all of them,' my Tua Kor instructed me.

'Can I have a piece too?' I asked, being greedy as usual.

'I just told you that we have just *cun cun,* enough for the pallbearers only,' replied my aunt impatiently. 'This stupid Choo Choo Kor, she never uses her brains. When I sent her out to order, she counted only the pallbearers. Anyway never mind, we will have the white bee koh to eat after we return from the funeral parlor.'

'Why is ours white and why do we have to eat this particular dessert?' I asked.

'Ours is white because that is the colour used for mourning,' Ah Gaik Chee replied on behalf of Tua Kor. 'Also when the deceased eat this kuih and he or she washes their hand, they will realize that they are dead.'

'How?' asked Geok Poh, who happened to be walking by and decided to join in our conversation.

'Well, when they wash their hands after eating this sticky dessert, one of their hands would be upturn and the other one would be down. That's how they know they are dead. Now go away don't disturb, we have a lot to do,' said Ah Gaik Chee as she pushed both Geok Poh and me out the kitchen door.

Monks from various temples were frequently coming and going, chanting every night beside the casket. Afterwards, guests were presented with a red packet filled with two hard candy and a red string before they go home. Apparently this was to wash off the bad luck and also to deter evil spirits from following them home.

The funeral does not mark the end of the rituals, for family members of the deceased are expected to mourn for a period of forty-nine days with prayers and offerings every seven days.

On the seventh day we were instructed to stay in our rooms at night and not wander around because that is the day my grandfather would return to the house for a visit. At the entrance of our bedroom door, I remember flour or talcum powder was sprinkled so we could determine if Ah Kong came home or not. If he did, his foot prints would show up on the flour or talcum powder. That night I made sure I did not drink water before bedtime. I definitely did not want to wake up in the middle of the night wanting to pee and meeting Ah Kong, should he return.

Another ritual surrounds the burning of hell money, a variety of paper goods such as large paper bungalow houses, TVs, sports cars, paper servant dolls and Bengali chauffeurs. I remember the Taoist priest that they invited to perform the ceremony. I remember crossing makeshift bridges, up down–up down before burning all the goodies for grandma.

Apparently, this was the first year rite, post-death ritual which also marked the end of our mourning period. After all was said and done, we were instructed to change into colourful clothing or at least some clothing, which had some red on it.

These events and images float vaguely in my mind, all I know for certain is never dress the deceased in red clothing. This will cause the spirit to come back as a ghost, and we definitely do not want that!!

# 15

# Looking After the Ashes

In the years following my grandfather's death, there were food offerings during different periods of time such as Cheng Beng (Tomb Sweeping Day), his death anniversary, or Ghost Month.

Coming home from school one day upon entering the door, I saw a temporary altar table set up facing the front of the house. Choo Choo Kor was filling an incense pot with uncooked rice for us to stick our joss sticks in after we prayed.

Jee Kor was arranging glasses of water in a row and some tea in small ceramic Chinese tea cups, and a teapot was placed on the table in front of the temporary 'incense pot.' On the corner of the altar table there was also a bamboo joss stick container that held new unused joss stick and a box of matches.

Ah Mah lit some joss sticks, then went to the front door, looking out into the porch. First she prayed to the God of Heaven and then prayed to 'invite' Ah Kong to come back to the house to feast.

Choo Choo Kor was instructed to open the side door to the house.

'Ah Mah, why do you need to open the side door and the front door?' I asked.

'That's where your Ah Kong's friends will enter,' replied my grandma, and then she went on acting busy, a sign that I should not ask any more questions.

Later on, Tua Kor explained to me that that's where Ah Kong's 'friends' would enter. This being Ah Kong's home, he could enter from the front door, but his friends, not being from this family, could not enter the living room through the front door because our deities' altar table was there.

The temporary altar table fascinated me because there were tons of food on it. There was also a small basin with a glass of plain water in it, and a face towel '*binpor*' that was folded and placed on top of the glass.

Ah Mah explained to me, 'The *binpor* is for Ah Kong to "cuci mulut, cuci muka", wash his mouth, wash his face before, after, and during eating.'

'Swee Lian, you are a good girl, one day when Ah Mah is no longer with you and you invite me to have a feast, please remember to offer me cigarettes and lau hiok (betel leaf), with gambier, and kaput (lime),' she reminded me with a smile showing off her dark yellowish-brown gambier-stained teeth.

The sirih that she eats on a daily basis also made her mouth red, as if it was covered in blood. It was quite *geli* (disgusting) yet amusing to watch her spit after chewing the betel nuts as well.

After she '*kao tai*,' left me instructions on what to do, she proceeded to make sure everything on the table was in perfect order.

Row one had eight pairs of chopsticks, where each is placed beside a saucer, which has a spoon and a small wine cup. Ah Kong liked to drink wine when he was alive, so Ah Mah insisted that wine must be served.

One thing that baffled me though was the chopsticks because we hardly ever used chopsticks in our daily life. We always used forks and spoons during meal times, or sometimes if I was with my mother, she would use her fingers to eat her meals.

Similarly we didn't drink tea in our daily life, but during this ritual, Chinese tea was served. During meals we seldom drank water and if we did, it would be plain cold water.

Looking at the second row, again my curiosity was piqued, but I did not dare ask my Ah Mah any more questions, so I turned to Jee Kor who was close by.

'Why are there eight bowls of rice, eight pairs of chopsticks, eight cups of wine, and eight cups of Chinese tea?' I asked. 'Is Ah Kong going to eat them all?'

'No, you silly girl, did you not remember, I told you that Ah Kong might bring along his friends? That is why we have to prepare more than one setting,' Jee Kor explained.

As soon as Jee Kor finished explaining, Ah Mah called to everyone in the household to come pray to Ah Kong, who apparently had arrived. How did Ah Mah know this? Remember the divination blocks that Ah Hwa Chee used in the temple? Well, Ah Mah used these same kidney-shaped wooden blocks that she called *puay* to ask yes/no questions to deities and ancestral spirits.

'Come, come faster, pray to Ah Kong,' ushered grandma in a hurried tone. Every family member lined up, and she would give us two joss sticks each to pray.

Why two and not one or three? According to Tua Kor's explanation it is because following the Yin principle when offering to the dead or ancestors are given we have to use even-number joss sticks. Odd numbers represent Yang numbers and thus used when offering to deities. That's something I need to remember, odd for deities, and even for ancestors or the dead.

During this time all my older cousins and my aunts would toil in the kitchen cooking the traditional Nyonya dishes. Chap chai mixed vegetables was one of them. Geok Poh and I normally squatted quietly beside the elders and watch in silence. Sometimes they would explain to us why they did certain things in a certain way, while other times they just kept quiet, concentrating on the task at hand.

For the chap chai, the dried lily buds were soaked and tied to a bunch. Jee Kor, who was in charge of this dish, explained that if the buds were not tied together before cooking them, the person would go astray after death.

Then there were other dishes like curry chicken and bangkuang char (fried Chinese turnip or jicama), and then there was a whole blanched duck and whole blanched chicken, yes with its head still attached and in their mouths were sprigs of spring onions. Then the rest I remember were various kinds of kuihs (desserts). There was also apples and oranges being offered. I knew Ah Kong liked apples, but I also knew he was not too fond of oranges. I guess Ah Mah must have added them because the orange colour symbolizes prosperity.

Cousin Geok Poh and I were most excited when Ah Kong 'finished eating' because this meant we could now eat the delicious food in front of us. To be certain that Ah Kong and his guests had finished and we could begin, Ah Mah would bring out the red wooden puay again and ask. Sometimes Ah Kong made fun of Ah Mah by having both puay land on the round sides, while other times he immediately answered 'yes' by landing one side up and one side down.

Growing up in my colourful household, I always knew I was different from the other non-Peranakan Chinese. Sometimes we were made fun of because we did not know how to speak Mandarin, well versed only in a mixture of English, Malay, and pseudo-Hokkien.

Memories of waking up next to white *bedak sejuk*-faced females sleeping beside you can be quite horrifying but nevertheless I would not trade the midnight storytellings of my older cousins before we went to sleep for anything. By the way, if you are wondering what 'bedak sejuk' is, it is a substance made of rice soaked in water, usually for weeks or even months, and left to ferment. After that, the rice is tediously washed and

grounded into white powder and made into tiny tablets. When we need to use it, all we have to do is put one tablet in the palm and put one or two drops of water. It will instantly melt the tablet into a paste and we then dab it on our faces. Supposedly this cooling powder can prevent pigmentation and also it is good for acne. To make them even more powerful, during the Mooncake festival, my aunts would place these rice pellets in a container on the table of offerings. They believed that by doing this, it would give transformative powers to the powder, making the user even more beautiful.

My grandmother, the matriarch of the family, and my aunts frequently had their hair tied up in tight buns called the *sanggul*. This look was completed by two long hair pins securing a third bun of fake hair, making them look rather fierce, but I knew in their hearts, they loved me very much. In spite of their lack of higher education, I believed my grandmother and my aunts to be very strong, powerful, and knowledgeable women.

Despite being surrounded by what one would classify as unproven old wives' tales, I still grew up feeling secure that if I were to fall sick and need help in any way, I could always rely on my Ah Mah or my aunts' help, and they would know what to do.

If I had a fever or felt unwell in any way, or perhaps I had an important exam or an interview coming up, they would not hesitate to bring me to the temple to consult a medium and get an angkong *hoo*, a Chinese talisman that is usually rectangular in shape, made from thin yellow paper with red Chinese words written on them.

The instructions on how to use them differed depending on the type of *hoo*. If these yellow strips of paper were a *peng-aun* hoo (a talisman that is meant for general health, emotional well-being and curing common ailments) then normally a prayer would be said before burning the *hoo* and dropping it into a glass of water for me to drink. If it was a *hoo* that was meant to protect the entire household then it would be brought home and pasted on doorways to ward off evil spirits.

I remember once when I was about ten years old. I was still in primary school and had fallen sick with the mumps. My glands were swollen, I looked like a basketball, and it was painful and uncomfortable. I could hardly open my mouth.

Tua Kor took one look at me and immediately knew what to do.

'Hurry up, Swee Lian, we want to arrive before the temple closes,' Tua Kor said impatiently. 'If we miss the consultation session today, we can't go tomorrow because there are no sessions held on Thursdays.'

'Which temple are we going to?' I asked as we were leaving the driveway.

'Don't ask so many questions, just rest. You will know when we arrive,' replied Tua Kor.

That day I was taken to the Tiger Temple or rather the temple with the tiger deity or deity sitting on tiger or deity with tiger spirit. Being a child who was not feeling too well and in some pain, all I knew was that it had something to do with tigers.

After about a fifteen-minute car drive we arrived. I was very relieved that, for once, the medium or priest who was supposed to treat me was not one of those scary ones that rolled their eyes and spoke in foreign tongues.

'Come, come little girl,' he beckoned to me. 'Sit down here,' he pulled up a plastic stool for me. 'Let Uncle take a look at you,' he continued kindly.

Throughout the examination he kept saying, 'No problem, no problem, can easily be cured, it's only the Pig Head Skin disease,' he smiled at me. 'Stay still ok? Now Uncle need to send a "tiger" in to eat up the pig,' he said as he picked up a Chinese brush dipped it into dark blue ink and wrote the Chinese character for tiger on the two swollen lumps on each side of my face.

'All done, the swelling should go down by tonight and in a couple of days you will be all better,' he assured me. He was right. Somehow, I recovered.

Yes, the swelling went down that very night and after a day or two, the pain was gone and my distorted face went back to its normal shape. Believe it or not!

Same thing happened when Mei Mei got the shingles. She was taken to an old 'uncle' who lived in a Siamese temple. He wasn't a priest or a medium, but he was allowed to live there because he had no family and was homeless. He also had this skill where he could *liak chua* (literally it means 'catch snakes' but in this case, it means to catch the shingles aka snake on the body).

Anyone with shingles would go to him and he would be able to heal them within days. I watched in amazement as this uncle chewed on some stuff and spit at my sister for a few times, covering her with his saliva and dark brown-looking bits and pieces. When she got home, her pain was gone, and within five days, so were her shingles.

Based on my own experience and what I had seen, at that time I truly believed that my Peranakan aunts and grandma were all very powerful. They had a cure, or could find one, for anything and everything. From straying husbands to healing broken hearts to acing exams to common illnesses, these women in my family seemed very confident of their remedy. And if they did not know the remedy, they would know who to take you to and get the remedy.

Over thirty years have passed since I last lived in that home. Various family members like my grandma, Tua Tneow, Tua Kor, and some servants have long passed away, but their 'warnings' still stick in my mind. Why? I suppose, I am the sum of all my family's parts.

Till this day I would not point at the moon lest it cuts my ear. In fact, at some point, I can't remember exactly when I did try to point just to prove that it was just a myth. I guess, based on my 'moon experiment' I chose not to challenge all the other 'warnings'.

I still do not whistle at night in case a ghost whistles back, I do not sit on pillows for fear that an angry boil would grow on my bottom, and I do not cut my nails at night because if spirits find my clippings it would allow them to take my place and that would shorten my life. When I was trying to conceive I sought the help of one of the 18 Louhans (Arhats) to ensure a healthy baby. And occasionally I still go to fortune tellers, especially when I am at a crossroads and unsure how to proceed with life. Keeping these old wives' tales alive somehow makes me feel connected to my loved ones. There is a sense of comfort that even though they have long passed on, they still look after me.

Do you have any superstitions that you still hold on to, even though they have no logic behind them? As for me, I know there are still many things from my childhood that follow and haunt me to this day, and not all of them are ghosts.